MURDER AT THE BED & BREAKFAST

A Liz Lucas Cozy Mystery - Book 4

BY

DIANNE HARMAN

Copyright © 2015 Dianne Harman

All rights reserved, including the right to reproduce this book, or portions thereof, in any form without written permission except for the use of brief quotations embodied in critical articles and reviews.

Published by: Dianne Harman
www.dianneharman.com

Interior, cover design and website by
Vivek Rajan Vivek
www.vivekrajanvivek.com

This is a work of fiction. Names, characters, places, and incidents either are the product of the author's imagination or are used fictitiously, and any resemblance to actual persons, living or dead, business establishments, events, or locales, is entirely coincidental.

ISBN: 978-1518622793

CONTENTS

	Acknowledgments	i
	Prologue	
1	Chapter One	1
2	Chapter Two	4
3	Chapter Three	6
4	Chapter Four	9
5	Chapter Five	11
6	Chapter Six	13
7	Chapter Seven	16
8	Chapter Eight	19
9	Chapter Nine	21
10	Chapter Ten	24
11	Chapter Eleven	28
12	Chapter Twelve	33
13	Chapter Thirteen	37
14	Chapter Fourteen	44
15	Chapter Fifteen	49
16	Chapter Sixteen	54
17	Chapter Seventeen	60
18	Chapter Eighteen	64

19	Chapter Nineteen	68
20	Chapter Twenty	73
21	Chapter Twenty-One	76
22	Chapter Twenty-Two	80
23	Chapter Twenty-Three	84
24	Chapter Twenty-Four	87
25	Chapter Twenty-Five	91
26	Chapter Twenty-Six	95
27	Chapter Twenty-Seven	101
28	Chapter Twenty-Eight	107
29	Chapter Twenty-Nine	111
30	Chapter Thirty	116
31	Chapter Thirty-One	120
32	Chapter Thirty-Two	127
33	Recipes	130
34	About Dianne	137

ACKNOWLEDGMENTS

Family, friends, people who email me and tell me how much they like my books – I'm indebted to all of you for your continuing support. It means so much to me.

I would be very remiss if I didn't thank the two people who make my books look so good, Tom Harman and Vivek Rajan. My husband Tom reads every word of every book several times looking for timeline problems, inconsistencies, and whatever else he feels the book needs or doesn't need. Believe me, without him, I'd be lucky to sell any books. Once the book is ready to be published it goes to Vivek. He's the one responsible for designing the fabulous covers and making sure that it all comes together in book form. It's a collaborative effort, and I so appreciate the time both of you put into making me a best-selling author.

Lastly, my thanks to you, my readers. Without you, I wouldn't be an author, and I never would have discovered my passion at a rather advanced age. I've never had so much fun! Again, thanks to each and every one of you!

Three Amazing Ebooks & Seven Paperbacks for FREE

Go to www.dianneharman.com/freepaperback.html and get your FREE copy of Kelly's Coffee Shop, Blue Coyote Motel and Dianne's favorite recipes immediately by joining her newsletter.

Once you join her newsletter you're eligible to win seven autographed paperbacks from the Cedar Bay Cozy Mystery Series. One lucky winner is picked every week. Hurry before the offer ends.

PROLOGUE

Laura wasn't surprised when she heard the soft knock on the bedroom door. She was the full time nanny for Bob and Renee Salazar's infant daughter, Celia, and she knew they'd be returning from the wedding and reception any minute. She opened the door expecting to see them, but instead, a person wearing a ski mask dressed entirely in black barged into the room.

She looked down and saw a gun in the intruder's hand that was pointed at her. Instinctively, knowing whoever it was meant to kill her, she positioned herself as far away as she could from the baby's crib. The last thing she heard was the pop of the gun; it's normally thundering sound softened by the silencer that had been attached to it. The baby, sensing something was wrong, began crying, scaring the killer, who quickly ran out the open door and down the hall, disappearing into the darkness of the night.

CHAPTER ONE

Liz Lucas stood by one of the large windows in her living quarters located on the lower level of the lodge looking out at the ocean. She was spending her last few hours as an unmarried woman quietly reminiscing about her past life and thinking about her new husband-to-be. The wedding was to be held within the next hour in the side yard next to the lodge. She smiled to herself as she thought about how well her children and Roger's, her future husband, had gotten along the previous evening.

Her daughter, Brittany, had flown in from Palm Springs, and her son, Jonah, from Dubai. By prearrangement they'd been met at the San Francisco airport by Roger's son, Jake, who had driven the two of them and his brother, Cole, to the spa and lodge located about sixty miles north of San Francisco. The four of them had become fast friends by the time they arrived at the spa.

The full family meeting the previous evening had gone very well, with all four children approving of their parent's future spouse. Liz and Roger had both been a little nervous about how the evening would go. Neither one of them had ever met the other one's children. Fortunately, it was a nonissue. All four of their children had one wish and one wish only, and it was that their respective parent would be happy. The prior spouses of Roger and Liz had died at an early age, and both of them had struggled with having lost someone they had dearly loved. It had not been an easy time for either of them, and their children were well aware of it.

Neither Liz nor Roger had ever thought they'd find someone they would want to marry. In fact, both of them had made a promise to themselves they would never marry again. As often happens, life has a way of intervening, and that's what happened when they met at Roger's law firm. Liz was there talking to the attorney who had handled the probate of her husband Joe's estate about a few loose ends that needed to be tied up. Roger was a senior partner in the law firm, and his specialty was criminal law. During the past few months he'd been invaluable in helping Liz solve a couple of murder mysteries in which she'd become involved.

Her reverie was broken by a quick knock on the door followed by her daughter bursting into the room. "Mom, it's time. I'm here to help you with your make-up and hair. Are you nervous?" Brittany asked.

"Yes, I'm terribly nervous. I simply can't believe I'm getting married. I really thought when your father died I would never remarry, yet here I am, about to walk down the aisle. In some ways I feel disloyal to Joe, but I know he'd want me to be happy."

"Well, if it's any consolation, Jonah and I are thrilled you're getting married. We really like Roger and his two sons. Come on, Mom, it's time. Jonah will never forgive me if I keep the bride from being on time, since he's giving you away. Think it's kind of cool that Jake is going to stand up for his dad," she said gently pushing Liz into a chair. "We talked briefly about who the other guests are, but let's go over them again. Fill me in while I help you with your make up."

"I think I told you when we first talked that the wedding was going to be very small. Just the immediate families and a couple of friends. I know you remember Judy, Tiffany's mother. She's driving up from San Francisco. Bertha, who I employ as my manager here at the lodge and spa, and her husband Hank, are coming. On Roger's side he's asked a friend of his, Bob Salazar, and his wife Renee. Roger and he became very good friends when they worked for the same law firm in San Francisco. Bob recently won an election as a county supervisor for Dillon County.

"They have a baby daughter, Celia. Renee's sister, Laura, is living with them. She's a nurse and when her last job ended, she decided to take them up on their offer of living with them and taking care of Celia so Renee could be more of a political wife and still have her psychology practice. The cottages here at the spa are only two to a room, so they're staying in a two bedroom suite at Cindy's Bed & Breakfast about a mile from here. That way there will be a separate bedroom for Laura and the baby."

"So that's it as far as who will be attending the wedding?"

"Yes, we only wanted a few people to attend."

"I think you told me you were expecting a lot of people at the reception."

"Sweetheart, this is a very small town. I've gotten to know a lot of the people in the three and a half years I've been here, plus, I've met a few more because of some murders I was involved in. I expect ..."

She was interrupted by Brittany. "What murders? You never said anything to me about any murders."

"Yes, that's true, but I didn't want to worry you, so I kept it to myself. Things just kind of happened, and I somehow became involved. Fortunately I had Roger to talk to and with his background in criminal law, he was invaluable to me. It all worked out, but let's talk about something else. I'm finished with murders."

Little did Liz know how untrue those words would soon turn out to be.

CHAPTER TWO

The first thing Nick Hutchinson did when he walked out the door of the Serene Valley Rehabilitation Center was call his ex-wife Laura.

"Hey, Laura, it's me, Nick. Just wanted you to be the first to know I made it through three months at the Rehab Center, and I'm clean as a whistle. I know I promised you a bunch of times that I'd quit using drugs, but this time it's for real. The doc at the Center said he'd never met anyone who had such a good outlook for the future. First thing I want to do is see you. I'll be at the house in about an hour."

He listened to Laura for a minute and then said in a raised and angry voice. "You're kidding! You mean to tell me I just spent three months of my life doing what you've been begging me to do for years, and now you're telling me it's too late. No, I don't think so, sweetheart, I'm on my way." He ended the call and got in his car, enjoying the feeling of freedom and knowing he would never have to take another drug test for the rest of his life.

What's wrong with that crazy broad? I do everything she asks, and then she tells me it's too late. That's crazy. She's never been able to resist me. Today won't be any different.

A moment later a little voice in his head that he hadn't heard for the past three months made itself known to him. "Why don't you call John?" the seductive silky voice asked. "After three months, you could use a little boost from something that will make you feel really good, and anyway, you're going right by his place on the way to Laura's."

What the heck. After three months of being on my best behavior, I deserve a little something. Probably would help the nervies I'm feeling. I've got this thing whipped, so a little of the good stuff John always keeps on hand couldn't hurt me. And anyway, if Laura had been nicer to me, I wouldn't need to do it. It's all her fault.

"John, it's Nick. Yeah, spent a little time at Serene. Figure I deserve a treat for getting out. I got this puppy whipped. Okay if I stop by?" He listened a minute. "On my way, man, thanks, and yeah, I want the good stuff."

CHAPTER THREE

Zack, the handyman at the spa, had made Liz promise to let him marry them when he heard she and Roger were getting married. He'd taken a course on the Internet and received a license which allowed him to conduct a marriage ceremony. As a handyman, he had a tendency to look a little shaggy. As a minister, he was very handsome and cleaned up well. His long black hair was tied back in a neat ponytail. He was cleanly shaven and wore a crisply ironed open-necked white shirt with black pants. Liz barely recognized him.

Next to him stood the groom-to-be, Roger Langley, along with his eldest son, Jake. His other son, Cole, was seated in one of the chairs that had been set out for the wedding guests. Brittany was Liz's maid of honor, and Jonah was giving her away. The guests were seated when Bertha started playing the song, "At Last" on the CD player in the lodge and then walked outdoors to take her seat. Jonah escorted a smiling Liz down the aisle between the chairs. She was radiant and wearing a cream-colored suit whose soft color contrasted well with her auburn hair and green eyes. Brittany privately thought they could have dispensed with anyone else being there, because it was apparent that Liz and Roger only had eyes for each other. Zack had clearly rehearsed his part and even gave a little "sermon" on the beauty of finding love again. Everyone who attended the wedding thought he might want to consider changing vocations and go into the ministry. Liz made a mental note to start looking for a new handyman.

"Who gives this woman in marriage?" Zack asked. He hadn't told them that he'd invited Liz's dog, Winston, to stand up with the couple. Liz and Roger grinned, looking at the big boxer who wore a cream-colored collar which matched Liz's silk suit.

"My sister and I do," a smiling Jonah said. Just as if he could understand everything that was being said, Winston barked, acknowledging he was giving his okay and allowing Roger to become a permanent fixture at the lodge and spa.

Zack took Liz's hand and placed it in Roger's hand while he put a ring on her finger. She did the same. After the exchange of rings, Zack said, "I now pronounce you man and wife. You may kiss the bride."

Although there were only a few people in attendance, their rousing clapping and joyous shouts sounded like a whole lot more people had attended the ceremony. Roger and Liz hugged each other as well as all of the guests. Bertha and her husband, Hank, went into the house and returned with champagne flutes and champagne.

"I didn't know we were going to have champagne before the reception," Liz said. "Bertha, you never told me you were doing this."

"As manager of the Red Cedar Spa and Lodge, I figure I can occasionally take some license with what I do here, and I definitely thought this was something that needed to be done." Hank filled the last of the glasses and Bertha turned to face Liz. "I'd like to make a toast. Everyone, please raise your glasses. To Liz and Roger, may you bring as much joy to each other as you bring to everyone else. We all wish you a long and happy marriage."

Everyone took a sip of champagne, and just then a plane towing a banner that said "I Love You, Liz," slowly flew overhead. Liz looked up, and the tears of joy she'd been holding back freely flowed down her cheeks.

"Oh, Roger, that's beautiful. Thank you so much."

The reception was being catered by the owner of Gertie's Diner located in Red Cedar. Gertie and several of her employees had been to the lodge earlier in the day to get ready for the reception. Now they began in earnest. A long table was set up next to the lodge with soft drinks, wine, and glasses.

The big cedar table in the great room of the lodge was groaning from the amount of food Gertie and her helpers put on it. Ovens were turned on and prepared food was taken out of the refrigerator. Spa employees arrived and helped carry chairs and tables out to the yard. Within a very short time, candles had been lit on the tables, wine was icing, and a large wedding cake was on a separate table in the great room. Cars filled with guests who had been invited to the reception began to fill the parking lot in front of the lodge. The reception began in earnest.

Just as Liz had predicted, a lot of townspeople attended the reception. Roger had recently opened a satellite office for his law firm next to Gertie's Diner, and almost all of his partners and their significant others attended the reception. Several other employees of the firm were there including Sean, who had been Roger's chief investigator when he was working in San Francisco and still helped him from time to time.

It was a joyous occasion, an occasion when two middle-aged people who were loved by many celebrated their wedding with friends and family.

No one could have predicted how the evening would end, least of all Roger and Liz. They would soon learn how short-lived happiness can be.

CHAPTER FOUR

The Reverend Lou Jacobs looked around his office in the rectory and fingered the cross that hung from a chain around his neck. He wore his black hair short so the grey at his temples gave him more credibility. Although he was in his mid-50's, he was still a very handsome man, and the Reverend Jacobs had no compunctions about using his good looks to appeal to the ladies in his congregation. He knew that some ministers felt they should dress humbly, but he'd never agreed with that philosophy. His monthly trips to the best clothing stores in San Francisco kept him looking as up-to-date as if he were a male model for a clothing company.

He thought about what he needed to do in the coming weeks to win the election. *I am so close. Just a couple more weeks, and I'll be the newest member of the Dillon County Board of Supervisors. Yes, Supervisor Jacobs sounds even better than Reverend Jacobs. I can smell the prize. This time I'm going to make it. The only thing standing in my way is that stupid little wetback, Bob Salazar.*

He picked up the phone on his desk and made a call. "Lester, it's Lou. Were you able to find out about Salazar's parents?" He listened for a moment. "You're absolutely sure that neither one of them is a legal citizen, and that they're definitely here illegally?" Again, he listened. "Okay. You got some proof, like a document or something? I need it for a hit piece I'm going to do on him. If you could bring it by right now, I'd appreciate it. Election's in two weeks, and I'd like to sew this up sooner rather than later."

Ten minutes later there was a knock on the door of his office. "Come in, Lester. Close the door behind you. I really don't want anyone else to know about this. I'm having a little holy water," he said, winking. "Would you care to join me?" He walked over to a table which had a small pitcher of what appeared to be water on it along with two glasses. He filled one up with vodka and handed it to Lester. "Cheers. Remind me when I'm the new county supervisor to find a place for you. I can always use a man like you in my organization. Let me see what you have."

Lester withdrew a folder from his briefcase, took out a piece of paper, and handed it to the reverend. The Reverend Jacobs spent a few moments looking it over and then put it down. "Thanks Lester, this is exactly what I need. Now I want you to make an anonymous phone call for me. I'm going to write down what I want you to say." He spent the next few minutes writing out a script for Lester to read when he made the phone call and then handed it to him.

After the call had been placed, and Lester had read his lines to perfection, the reverend said, "It's probably better if you leave now. Since I'm sure my opponent will be withdrawing from the race, I'm pretty much a shoe-in. See you at the election night party, and I'm having a special little party after that for some of my people. You're invited. Some of my friends from San Francisco are coming up for it and will provide a little entertainment, if you know what I mean. They do mean things with their tassels. Think you'll enjoy it. Thanks for bringing me the winning ticket."

CHAPTER FIVE

Not a day goes by that I don't miss Don, Nancy thought. *He was everything to me. We were soulmates, just like you read about in the supermarket tabloids. I know he was married to Camille for a few years and had two children by her, but once we met there was never anyone else for either of us. He was the most wonderful man in the world. He was my hero, a man who knew what was right and what was wrong with the United States, and now he's gone.*

Don had two daughters, Laura and Renee, and she remembered when Renee told him she was going to marry Bob Salazar. Don had become almost apoplectic at the mere thought that a daughter of his would marry a Mexican. He was a firm believer that all Mexicans should be sent back to where they came from. He still resented President Bush for not sealing the borders and thereby allowing them to flood into the United States, taking jobs that belonged to red, white, and blue Americans.

Nancy knew how hurt he'd been when Renee had told him about the forthcoming marriage. She remembered him saying, "It was bad enough when Laura married a good-for-nothing drug addict, but I had higher hopes for Renee. She could have had her pick of men, including that wealthy rancher, Mitch Warren, who she was engaged to." What had added insult to injury in Don's eyes was that Bob Salazar was twenty years older than Renee, fifty years to her thirty, and only a few years younger than Don. The days following Renee's announcement had not been easy ones for either Don or Nancy. He had vacillated between being furious and being severely depressed. She'd finally insisted he make an appointment with his doctor and get some medication to help him through his ordeal.

It was as if something died in Don from the moment Renee had told him about it. He lost interest in everything having to do with the government, and whenever a Mexican or a Hispanic was on television he turned it off, even if it was one of the players on his favorite baseball team, the San Francisco Giants. Food no longer interested him, and he spent hours in bed, often not getting up until late in the afternoon, if at all. Although Don didn't do anything as obvious as hold a gun to his head or swallow poison, it became apparent to Nancy he'd made his mind up that he wanted to die.

Renee asked Don to give her away at the wedding, but he refused to even attend and never spoke to her again. When he found out she was pregnant and that he was going to be the grandfather of a half-Mexican grandchild, he vowed to die and so he did. Laura was the one who had told him about Renee's pregnancy, and she'd also told him she was going to be the baby's nanny and live with Bob and Renee. Nancy was certain Laura was responsible for Don's death. It had been several months now since Don's death, and she hated Laura with every fiber in her being, blaming her for killing Don.

Nancy didn't know how she was going to get back at Laura, only that she had to do something to avenge Don's death. She couldn't bring herself to kill his grandchild, and he'd always told her that privately, Renee was his favorite, so she couldn't bring herself to kill Renee either, but in her mind Laura's death could be justified. After all, wasn't she the one who ultimately was responsible for Don's death? Although she knew it could never be proven in a court of law, she felt she alone knew the truth - that Laura was responsible for Don's death. And shouldn't she also die for what she had done? In Nancy's twisted mind, the answer was a resounding absolutely, positively yes!

CHAPTER SIX

It was early evening when the guests began to leave, the last ones being Bob and Renee. It was a rare event when they were alone without their newborn daughter, Celia. The politicians and attorneys that seemed to always need to talk to Bob. They'd thoroughly enjoyed the wedding and reception. Liz had spent quite a little time with Renee and considered her to be a new friend. She'd told Renee she'd very much like her to be a guest at the spa before they went home the next day, and Renee had eagerly accepted her invitation.

"Hon," Gertie said, walking over to Liz with a large tray of appetizers as she was getting ready to leave. "Ya' gotta try these pizza twirls I came up with 'em jes' fer yer' weddin'. Everybody's tellin' me they're the best thing since sliced bread. Probably gonna have to put 'em on the menu at the diner. Also bet yer' gonna want the recipe, so you can fix 'em for yer' spa guests at the nightly dinners ya' give 'em. Bet ya' can't eat jes' one!"

Liz knew once Gertie wanted you to try something, there was no way to get out of it. She took one of the appetizers from the tray and popped it in her mouth. "You weren't kidding, Gertie. These are fabulous. Yes, I definitely want the recipe. Thank you so much."

"My pleasure, darlin'. Yer' worth it," Gertie said..

Liz and Roger thanked Gertie and her staff. When they were gone, their four children once again told them how happy they were for Liz and Roger. As they walked to their cottages they made their way past Brandy Boy, who was in his customary place on the porch, waiting for the little ding-ding-ding of the bell from one of the cottages. His sole purpose in life was to deliver a wee bit of brandy to the guest who was staying there and then be rewarded with a dog treat.

"Brandy Boy, give me a minute, and I promise I'll ring the bell for you. I've only read about you, but I definitely want to see you in action," Jake said laughing. "Dad's told me all about your deliveries, and I can't come to the lodge without seeing the dog that's been all over television and in all the papers do his shtick!" Brandy Boy never acknowledged him or moved.

Roger closed the door behind him and walked over to Liz, hugging her. "Well, it's just you and me now, Mrs. Langley. Better get used to it. I've never been happier."

"Nor have I, but I think you're forgetting something," she said, looking down at the big dog who had a paw up, almost in defeat. "I don't think it's just you and me. With Winston, I think it's more like we three. Hope you don't mind."

Roger pulled away and reached down, petting the big boxer. "Don't worry, boy, you're part of the family, but I would like to kiss the bride, if you don't mind."

He had just put his arms around Liz, enveloping her in a hug, when his cell phone, which he'd left on the kitchen counter, rang.

"Roger, whoever it is, it can wait. We're entitled to our time together. After all, this is our day."

"Everyone knows today's the wedding, but I want to check and make sure it's not an emergency. Hmm," he said, looking at the monitor. "It's Bob Salazar. I better see what he wants. I'll just be a minute, and then we can resume where we left off." He picked up the phone. "Hi, Bob, what's so important that it can't wait until tomorrow. I assume you do know this is my wedding day considering you left here only a few minutes ago."

Roger listened for a moment and then said, "Don't do anything. We're on our way." He ended the call and turned to Liz, "Someone killed Renee's sister. We have to go to Cindy's Bed & Breakfast right now." He ran downstairs to get his gun from the top drawer of his bureau.

Liz opened the door and asked Roger what had happened as they ran to his car. "All I know is that he was pretty emotional. Evidently Cindy heard their baby, Celia, crying far longer than was normal for her. Laura usually picked her up, and she would stop crying after a couple of minutes. Cindy was concerned something had happened and knocked on the door of the room where Celia and Laura were staying. There was no answer, so she went in and discovered that Laura had been shot and was obviously dead. She grabbed the baby and was trying to calm her down when Bob and Renee got there a few moments later. That's all I know."

"Why didn't Cindy hear a gun shot and report it?"

"I had the same thought. The killer must have used a silencer."

"Poor Renee. She told me she was so happy that she and Laura were becoming close again. Evidently they had been estranged for a while, something about Renee not approving of Laura's ex-husband. Laura recently divorced him and since she was a nurse out of a job, it seemed like a perfect solution to have her take care of Celia while Renee tried to balance her psychology practice while helping with Bob's election campaign."

"Seems like the police haven't been called yet. I don't see any red and blue flashing lights or that buffoon police chief's car. We should know more in a few minutes." Lights spilled out of every window. As Roger pulled into the circular driveway of Cindy's Bed & Breakfast, he said, "Even if the police haven't been called, it looks like all the guests know what has happened. Great way to start a honeymoon, Mrs. Langley, sorry." They threw the car doors open and ran up the steps to where Bob was waiting for them on the porch.

CHAPTER SEVEN

After Bob had ended his call to Roger he paused for a few moments thinking about the events of the last few weeks. Renee hadn't understood why he'd withdrawn from the campaign for county supervisor after spending the last year actively pursuing it. She'd asked him several times why he'd changed his mind, and each time he told her the same thing - he'd decided now that they had a child he wanted to spend more time with Renee and Celia. Renee suspected there was more to it than that, but Bob had been adamant that spending time with his family, rather than taking care of county business, was far more important to him.

He'd pulled out of the race late in the afternoon after he'd received the anonymous call threatening to expose his parents as illegal immigrants. Bob's parents had come to the United States illegally and had eventually made their way to California's Central Valley. They were very frugal and even though they had six children, they were able to save and buy land to grow the produce that grew so easily in that area of the state. Within several years, they'd managed to buy hundreds of acres and hired friends and family to work the land. Bob's parents had impressed upon him from an early age that he was the smart one in the family, and that he had to get a college education. They didn't want to see their son, who seemed to be so intelligent, working on the land. It was all right for their other children, but not for Bob, or Roberto, his legal name.

Their faith in him had been well-placed. He excelled in high school and received a scholarship to the University of California. He graduated with honors and then attended law school at the University of California, Berkeley. The fact that he was a Latino hadn't hurt when he'd applied and also probably helped him qualify for the full scholarship he received from the law school scholarship fund. He didn't know if it was his ethnicity or his academic record that had been responsible for the full scholarship, but he gladly accepted the financial benefits it provided.

When Bob was in college, he became aware that as illegal immigrants his parents were in a tenuous situation, and the Border Patrol could deport them to Mexico. Since all of their children had been born in the United States, they were legal U.S. citizens, but his parents' status was always only one knock away on the door in the middle of the night from being sent back to Mexico. When he first brought up the subject of becoming U.S. citizens to them, his parents gave him all of their reasons why they didn't want to become U.S. citizens.

As the years went on, the subject was met with deaf ears and silence. He finally realized they felt they were in a Catch-22 situation. If they told anyone they were illegal immigrants, they were certain their land would be taken from them. Although it wasn't true, someone had once told them that, and no amount of explaining on Bob's part could get them to change their mind on the subject. After numerous attempts at trying to persuade them otherwise, he'd given up and just hoped no one ever found out his parents were in the United States illegally.

When the phone call had come several weeks ago telling Bob that if he didn't drop out of the race his parents would be exposed as illegal immigrants, he'd spent several hours anguishing over what he should do. He knew Renee would urge him to stay in the race and let the chips fall where they may. He also knew he couldn't allow his parents to be exposed as illegal immigrants. The stakes were just too high for him to do that. If it hadn't been for their support and encouragement, he'd be just another Mexican working in the fields and living from paycheck to paycheck rather than a wealthy attorney in a private practice with a wife he adored and an infant daughter. Late that afternoon he'd called a press conference and dropped out of the race, citing as his reason that he wanted to spend more time with his young growing family.

Neither he nor the reverend he was running against nor anyone else could have foreseen the strange outcome of the election. It had been too late to remove his name from the ballot since it had already been printed, and he had won the race by an overwhelming majority. The talking heads wagged about it for days and Bob, being the honorable man he was, decided that if the public felt that strongly about his being elected as a Dillon County Supervisor he had no choice but to accept the position.

He didn't know how or why, but he was sure his sister-in-law, Laura, had been murdered because he'd made the wrong decision and decided to accept the job of county supervisor after winning the election by a landslide.

The more he thought about it, the more convinced he became that Laura's murder was a vendetta against him for becoming the new Dillon County Supervisor. Having his sister-in-law murdered because of him was the worst experience of his life, and if Renee ever found out that Laura had probably been murdered because of him, he knew she'd leave him and his life wouldn't be worth living. Falling in love with Renee and marrying her had been the most wonderful experience of his life, and he didn't want to lose her.

CHAPTER EIGHT

"Bob, I am so sorry. This is absolutely shocking and beyond belief. How's Renee doing? Is Celia all right?" Roger asked, after he sprinted up the steps of the bed and breakfast to where Bob sat in a porch chair, his arms crossed, seemingly in shock.

"Roger, I can't believe this," Bob said, looking up at Roger." Who would want to kill Laura? She was one of the sweetest, most loving people I've ever known. As far as Renee - she's devastated. She and Cindy are taking turns comforting Celia and trying to calm her down. Fortunately she's too young to know what happened, but I wonder if she'll be traumatized by it at some level. She was really attached to Laura, and I'm sure she'll miss her. She's just too young to verbalize it. What should I do now? You're the expert in criminal law."

"First of all you need to call Seth Williams. He's the police chief in Red Cedar. He's a bumbling idiot, but he is the chief, plus he's indebted to Liz and me. Since I know him, it would probably be best if I called him." He took his phone out of his pocket and pressed in the police chief's phone number.

"Seth, it's Roger Langley. Yeah, I enjoyed the reception too. Unfortunately, this is a business call. The sister-in-law of a good friend of mine has been murdered. We're at Cindy's B & B. I need you to come right away."

He ended the call and turned to Bob. "He'll be here momentarily. First of all, I need to know who would want Laura dead. Naturally, the place to begin is with Laura. I'm thinking relationships, people who might not like her, that type of thing. What about Laura's ex-husband? Liz mentioned him on the way over. Secondly, would anyone want to hurt you or Renee? Is someone trying to get at you through your sister-in-law? You're a Dillon County Supervisor now. Any problems there?

"I've never asked you before, but have you previously been married? Are there any disgruntled employees or clients, either in your current law practice or when you were with the firm in San Francisco who might want to retaliate against you? Is there anything you can think of at all? And like I always tell my clients - who has the most to gain from Laura's death?"

Bob put his head in his hands. After several minutes, he looked up at Roger and said with a vacant look in his eyes, "I honestly can't think of anyone who would profit from Laura being dead or would want to see her dead."

"I don't know anything about Renee's past. How did you meet her? Was she involved with someone else. Has she previously been married? In other words, if someone wanted to get at Renee through Laura, who would it be?"

"From the moment I found out that Laura had been murdered, I've been asking myself the same question, and I just can't come up with anyone."

"Tell me more about Renee. I really like her, but I sure don't know much about her."

CHAPTER NINE

In a hesitant and emotional tone of voice, Bob started to speak. "I met Renee at a Republican political event. As you know, when I left the firm where you and I worked together in San Francisco, I opened up a law office in Dillon, which is pretty much in the middle of the county. I'd thought for a long time that we need more Latinos in politics and had pretty much made a decision to get into county politics. I attended several county Republican political party meetings, and a man at one of the meetings befriended me. He urged me to become involved and told me he would introduce me to the movers and shakers in the county.

"Renee comes from a wealthy family in the area. Her father and stepmother lived in Red Cedar, and he was once the mayor. He had a large ranch and sold it to a developer, then he made a ton of money playing the stock market. Even though Renee was originally from here, she moved to Dillon when the opportunity came to take over a retiring psychologist's practice. We happened to see each other a number of times at various different Dillon events, and one night I was seated next to her at a political event. The rest is history. She'd been engaged for some time to a rancher, although they hadn't set a date. Renee broke her engagement to him, and from that moment on we were together.

"Her father was very opposed to our relationship. He considered me to be nothing more than a wetback and unfortunately, because of me, he and Renee became estranged. He had been divorced from Renee's mother, Camille, for a long time, and his new wife went along with him and terminated her relationship with Renee. Renee's mother accepted me with open arms, and we became very close."

"What about that rancher who was engaged to Renee? Where is he now? Did he find someone else? Would the fact that Renee broke off her relationship with him cause him to be a suspect? And what about her father? Although it's hard for me to think of a father killing one daughter to get back at another."

"Nor can I, plus there's the fact that her father died several months ago. It was a very difficult time for Renee, because she and her father had never reconciled. As for the rancher, he's still around. I haven't seen him in quite awhile, but immediately after Renee and I started going together, if we ran into one another, he always made a point of ignoring me. To my knowledge, he hasn't found anyone else, but I could be wrong. I just don't know much about him. Once Renee broke off the engagement, I didn't think there was any reason for me to have anything to do with him, and it was obvious he wanted nothing to do with me. Can't say I blame him."

"What about Laura? Anything in her past that would indicate a problem? A problem important enough that someone would want to see her dead?"

"My sister-in-law was one of the nicest people I've ever known. She was a nurse by profession and was a caregiver in every sense of the word." He paused for a moment nearly overcome by grief and then continued. "Maybe she was too much of a caregiver. She recently divorced her husband. He was a good-for-nothing. It was always Renee's opinion that Laura thought she could rehabilitate him. He was a drug addict. She begged him to go to a recovery center, but he refused. After she divorced him, he finally did seek treatment. I don't know if he's still in rehab or not."

The screen door opened and Liz walked out. "I'm sorry, Bob, but I couldn't help but overhear your conversation with Roger. Roger's the expert here, but sure sounds to me like there are some suspects, like Laura's ex-husband and Renee's ex-fiancé for starters. I see the police chief's car coming. I don't want to tell you your business, but it might be a good idea not to tell him what you just told Roger. Tact and diplomacy are not his specialties. Actually, I've had to get involved in a couple of murders that have happened lately around this area, and if you don't mind, I'd like to help you. Roger and I were planning on spending this week in Red Cedar anyway. Because of the wedding, we closed the lodge for a week, so I don't have to cook for guests. Can you find out the name of the recovery center where Laura's ex-husband was getting his rehab treatment? I think that's as good a place as any to start."

Renee walked out just as Liz finished talking, tears streaming down her cheeks. Bob walked over to her and wrapped his arms around her, "Sweetheart, I am so sorry. Laura didn't deserve this."

She pulled out of his embrace. "Her ex-husband's name is Nick Hutchinson, and he's been in the Serenity Center for treatment of his drug abuse. Whether he's still there or not, I don't know. I remember he called Laura the night before he decided to enter it to let her know he wanted to get clean and start over with her. She told me at the time that she had led him on and told him maybe they could get back together after he got clean. Actually, Laura had no intention of having anything more to do with him, but she was afraid if she told him that, he wouldn't go in for treatment.

"She knew it would be the best thing for him, and quite frankly, I couldn't have agreed more with her. I've worked with addicts, and a lot of them feel if there's something to be gained by seeking help, they will. Often the fact that a loved one will take them back or they'll reconcile with people close to them is enough motivation for them to turn their lives around. If he's the one who killed her, it's my fault, because it was at my urging that Laura gave him hope that they might reconcile."

Once again, tears poured down Renee's stricken face, trying to come to grips with the fact that if Laura's ex-husband was the murderer, she may have inadvertently given him a reason to kill her.

CHAPTER TEN

The black and white police car came to a skidding stop in front of the steps leading to the porch of Cindy's Bed & Breakfast. The car door flew open, and Seth Williams, the ruddy-faced chief of police, had to use his hands to manually move his huge belly from the center of the steering wheel to the left of it so he could get out of the car.

Liz had noticed earlier at the wedding reception that Seth's customary breakfast spill of eggs from Gertie's Diner was on his shirt, and it was obvious he hadn't changed his clothes since then.

"Hey Liz, Roger, congrats. Bet your kids are happy you made it legal. Even though most young people these days live together and cohabitate like rabbits, they ain't usually too happy when their parents do the same thing. So where's the stiff?" Seth asked in his usual less than tactful way.

Bob and Renee stared at him, having a hard time understanding how anyone could be so insensitive.

"Laura's in the bedroom at the far end of the hallway," Cindy said, opening the front door of the bed and breakfast for Seth.

"Cindy, good to see 'ya, altho ya' could probably do without someone gettin' knocked off at yer' B & B. People get real squeamish 'bout sleepin' in a room where someone's been offed. Called Wes, the county coroner, and he should be here any minute. Tol' him to bring the wagon, that I had a delivery fer him." He turned to Liz. "Ya' know yer' purty good at solvin' these types of crimes, but gotta tell ya', sure is strange we never had no murders 'til ya' got involved. Ya' gonna' try to solve this here one?"

"I have no idea. If I do you'll be the first to know."

"Well, since I'm the chief of police in this here town, darn tootin' I should be the first to know," he said hitching up his pants over his massive belly as he waddled down the hall to the bedroom where Laura had been murdered.

A few minutes later a white van pulled up behind Seth's police car, and a middle-aged man opened the door and got out of it. "Liz, Roger, that was a wonderful reception today, but this sure isn't the best way to start out your new life together as a married couple. When Seth called he said it was the sister of one of your friends."

"Yes," Liz said. "Her name is Laura Hutchinson. She's in the bedroom at the end of the hall. Seth is in there now."

Wes rolled his eyes towards heaven and muttered something to himself. He turned to Liz and said, "I hope you're going to get involved. We all know Seth couldn't find his way out of a paper sack. Let me be the first of many in our community to say I think your talents are needed here."

"Wes, I'll be happy to see what I can find out. I've done Seth a couple of favors, so I don't think he'd mind if I got involved."

"Mind?" he said over his shoulder as he walked down the hall. "I would think he'd be forever grateful. He's not the most perceptive man in the world, but even he knows that you have some sort of sixth sense about these things. I remember you once called it a niggle. Hope your niggle helps you find out who did this."

"Thanks, Wes." Liz said. "I don't think there's any more we can do here tonight, and I'm sure our kids wonder what happened to us. Probably time for us to head back to the lodge."

"I'm so sorry to have bothered you on your wedding night," Bob said, "but I didn't know who else to call."

"It's not a problem, Bob. You did the right thing," Liz said as she walked over to Renee. "I'll call you tomorrow. If you or Bob think of anything else, even if it's something really inconsequential, but might have some bearing on this murder, please call me."

Roger shook Bob's hand and hugged Renee. "Try and get some sleep. There's nothing more you can do tonight, and I'm sure Celia needs you. You're a psychologist. While she may not consciously be aware of what's happened, unconsciously she may feel that something's wrong, and she could probably use some mommy and daddy time."

Cindy walked them out to their car. "Liz, I know you've had good luck solving three recent murder cases here in Red Cedar. I remember how worried you were about your spa's reputation when the mayor's wife was murdered in one of the cottages at the spa. Well, I feel the same way. The reputation of my B & B is at stake here. I've worked really hard to make a go of it, and I sure don't want to see it go under because someone happened to get murdered here. Much as I can't stand that oafish police chief, he's absolutely right. To quote him, 'People get real squeamish 'bout sleepin' in a room where someone's been offed' even if the B & B and I had nothing to do with it. I sure would like for you to find out who did it."

"I'll do my best, I promise. I understand exactly what you're going through."

Liz and Roger got in his car and drove the short distance back to the spa. When they got there, every light in the lodge and spa was on. Liz turned to Roger, "What's going on? This is very strange. I can understand the lights being on in the cottages, but look at this," she said gesturing towards the lodge.

As they parked his car in front of the lodge, Bertha and Hank walked out. "Liz, Roger, Seth called and told us about Bob's sister-in-law. He said maybe someone had a vendetta against the owners of places to stay in the area and advised me to turn on all the lights."

"You've got to be kidding. I don't think Laura's murder had anything to do with the spa, but thanks anyway. Hank, go on and take Bertha home. It's been a long day for all of us. I really appreciate you coming back here and doing this, but I don't think there will be a problem. We'll turn the lights off."

"All right, if you're sure. I know you told me and the spa staff to take this week off, but given the murder, would you like me back here tomorrow morning? I'm not sure what I can do to help, but there must be something. Oh, one other thing. We may be losing Zack. Every one told him he did such a wonderful job today officiating at your wedding that he mentioned to me he just might go to seminary school and become a minister. I told him he'd have to give up his love affair with beer, and he said that wouldn't be a problem. He told me he felt like he'd had a calling from the 'Big Man' upstairs and he couldn't ignore it."

"I'm having a hard time wrapping my mind around Zack becoming a minister, although I agree, he acted today like it was the most natural thing in the world for him. Wouldn't that be ironic? He and I talked about me needing someone to conduct the ceremony and he volunteers and then becomes a minister and leaves his employment here the spa. Couldn't have scripted that one. Good night and thanks again for everything you did today."

CHAPTER ELEVEN

"Mrs. Langley," Roger said, "there are a lot of things I would like to do to celebrate our wedding, but I think the first thing we need to do is feed the dog of honor and the lodge mascot. After that, we can talk about what steps we should take to investigate this case and where we should start. Maybe it's a good thing we both took this week off. It certainly isn't the way I wanted to start out our marriage, but you know what a good friend of mine Bob is, and it's pretty obvious he needs our help given the fact that Chief Williams is totally incompetent."

"Oh, Roger. I feel so sorry for Renee. It's bad enough to have your sister murdered, but to have your baby daughter witness it makes it doubly hard. Naturally the baby doesn't know what happened because of her age, but I'm sure it's had an emotional impact on Renee, thinking that her daughter was a witness to a murder. It's a good thing she's a psychologist, because something like that is bound to make you feel guilty. Think about it. She and Bob are having a wonderful time at our wedding and reception while a mile away her sister's being murdered, and their daughter is a witness." Liz crossed her arms and rubbed her shoulders, shivering as she thought of the evilness of what had happened.

Roger walked over and hugged her. "Are you all right?"

"Yes, I'm fine. It's just so sad, and I hate that it happened during our reception. That's going to be hard for both of us to ever forget."

"You're looking at the situation as if the glass is half empty. The glass half full approach is we're here for Bob and Renee, and we don't have to work this week." Roger prepared dinner for the two dogs. "Brandy Boy, Winston, come." He set Winston's dish down on the kitchen floor and took Brandy Boy's dish out to the porch. The only time Brandy Boy left the porch was in the evening when a guest wanted a shot of brandy delivered to his cottage by the big dog. Other than that he was a permanent staple on the porch. A raised eyelid when someone walked by him was the only indication that the dog was aware of anything other than the ding-ding-ding of a cottage bell being rung.

"Liz," Roger said when he stepped back in the lodge after feeding Brandy Boy. "I'd like to make a list of possible suspects based on what Bob told us and also a list of what we need to do and things we need to find out." He walked downstairs and returned with two yellow legal pads and pens.

"Okay, let's start. First thing we need to find out is if Laura's ex-husband is still in Serenity Center or if he's checked out," Roger began.

"Let me do that. I've met the director of the center a couple of times, and I think he'll remember me."

"Okay, you're on. I'll look into that rancher Renee was engaged to."

"Fine by me. Do you know his name?" Liz asked.

"No. I'm not sure Bob even knows his name, or he could have been so overwrought with grief when he told me about him this evening that his name simply escaped him."

"I'll call Renee early tomorrow morning, before they leave, and find out," Liz said. "I told her I'd call, so it won't seem too strange that I'm asking some questions."

"Bob told me Renee's father and Renee had become completely estranged when she and Bob decided to get married."

"I remember meeting him once. I think he was the mayor of Red Cedar years ago. Is he still alive?" Liz asked.

"No. Bob told me he'd died a few months ago."

"Well, I don't think much of that angle. Since her father is deceased, I don't see how he could in any way, shape, or form be involved in the murder of his daughter. And anyway, since he disapproved of Renee marrying Bob, I would think if he was going to have a daughter killed, it would be Renee, not Laura."

"You're probably right." Roger became very quiet, obviously deep in thought.

"I can see that's something you'd still like to explore. When I talk to Renee tomorrow morning, I'll ask her more about the family situation. Maybe there's something, although I don't know what it could be." She made a note on her legal pad and looked up at Roger. "We're concentrating on Renee and Laura. What about Bob?"

"I was getting to him. Although Bob and I didn't have time to discuss everything at length earlier this evening, there are some things that have been going through my mind. I'm wondering about Bob announcing a couple of weeks before the election that he was dropping out of the race, and then when he won the race, even though he'd dropped out, he took the job. He never told me what that was all about. Maybe the political thing has something to do with the murder."

"Roger, I remember you telling me his opponent had run for that office a couple of times before and lost. Could he have been so desperate to win he did something to keep Bob from running? Or maybe he was so angry he lost the election he decided to get back at Bob? How would he do it? He kills Laura, a close family member of Bob's."

"I don't know. The only thing I know about his opponent is that he's a minister of a very conservative church. That's pretty much all Bob told me. I'll talk to Bob, and see if I can find out something."

"Was Bob romantically involved with anyone before Renee? Was he divorced? What was his marital status?"

"I don't know that either. He never introduced me to anyone, and we were pretty good friends when he was working with me at the San Francisco law firm."

"Why did he leave?" Liz asked.

"He told me the only cases the law firm seemed to give him were the ones that involved Latinos or Mexicans. He thought the reason they did that was because he was Mexican. Bob really resented it. He said he felt like he was the firm's token Mexican, and he didn't like it. One time he complained to me that he hadn't gone to Cal Berkley's School of Law on a full scholarship so he could be a firm's poster boy for supporting minority employment."

"And yet he was willing to put his Mexican heritage in the limelight when it came to politics," Liz mused. "Seems like those are polar opposites."

"I could be wrong, but I think Bob felt that if he was going to be the poster boy for some law firm, their token Mexican so to speak, he would rather start his own law office where he could make the decisions about what types of cases to take. I think he's very sincere in his desire to see more Mexicans have a say in politics, particularly since they're now a majority of the population here in California. As for being a poster boy for the Republican Party, I think he felt if he could be a voice for the Mexicans in this state he'd be happy to do it. It's just my feeling, but I believe anyone with his good looks, intelligence, and educational background would certainly be effective in issues important to Latinos."

"Did he ever talk about going to the state or national level in politics?"

Roger thought for a minute. "Recently we were having a cup of coffee, and I told him about a client of mine who had an issue with the county. I wanted to get his input, because he was the only county supervisor I knew. He happened to mention he had a feeling he was being considered to be an up and comer by the national party, and that he'd been asked to speak to several political groups outside the state."

"I know it's a stretch, but do you think his Mexican heritage could have played some part in Laura's murder?"

"I have no idea," Roger said, "but I've learned over the years not to leave any stone unturned. I'll ask him about that angle as well when I speak to him tomorrow." He stood up and picked up his notepad. "Mrs. Langley, enough of this for tonight. We have about twelve hours before we can do anything more on this case. Personally, I'd like to make them count. After all it is our wedding night," he said, grinning as he turned off the lights and they walked down the stairs towards the bedroom.

CHAPTER TWELVE

It's all her fault I have to live my life from pill to pill. They're the only things that keep me from becoming severely depressed again, but I'm sure not happy, and I know I never will be again.

Mitch Warren stood in front of the large living room window that overlooked the Lazy K Ranch. The late evening apricot sky was slowly shifting into blue, the precursor of the coming darkness of night. The lush green grass of the large front yard stood in sharp contrast to the freshly painted white picket fence that lined the lane that led to the ranch house. In the distance he saw a herd of his cattle as they grazed contentedly in the pasture, and closer to the ranch house he admired the barns that housed the horses. All in all, it was a very bucolic setting. No matter how many times he looked at the land that had been in his family for generations, he never tired of it.

His shoulders sagged as he turned away from the window and thought for the thousandth time about how Renee would have been perfect as his partner, his wife, in taking care of the land for future Warren generations to enjoy. It had been two years now, and he still couldn't believe she'd broken off her engagement to him and for that guy who was a relative newcomer to Dillon County. He shook his head, still having a hard time believing what had happened.

Mitch and Renee had known each other since high school. She'd been the homecoming queen, and he'd been president of the senior class. They had gone on to college, Renee to the University of California at Berkeley, much to her conservative father's dismay, and Mitch to Stanford. He'd wanted to marry her when they graduated from college. After all, it was a foregone conclusion they'd get married at some point. He was ready for it to happen right after college.

She'd refused, saying she wanted to get her psychology practice established first. The years went by, Mitch expanding the ranch by buying adjoining lands, and Renee developing a thriving psychology practice. Not a year had gone by that Mitch had not talked about getting married and urging Renee to set a date. She finally placated him by accepting an engagement ring from him. Her father was just as adamant that it was time for them to get married. For whatever reason, Renee continued to stall.

Renee became interested in county politics and was very involved in helping the local county Republican Party however she could, over time working her way up to county vice-chair of the party. Politics had never interested Mitch, and he had a hard time understanding her fascination with it. He still blamed politics for what happened to their relationship. He never knew the particulars, but what he did know was that one night he received a call from Renee asking him to meet with her. The next thing he knew, she was apologizing for not being able to marry him and handing him back the engagement ring she had worn for several years. She told him she hoped they'd be able to remain friends.

The next few months were the worst of Mitch's life. Not only had Renee broken up with him, but he soon learned that she was going to marry a man who was very involved in county politics by the name of Bob Salazar. Almost a year later family members insisted he seek professional help for treatment of his depression. The psychiatrist he'd been seeing in San Francisco recommended that he check himself into a mental hospital for treatment of his acute depression, which he did. The only non-family visitor during that time was Renee's father. They had become very close over the years, probably because of their very strong conservative views.

As the months went by his attitude towards Renee began to change, and he began to hate her for what she had done to him - very simply breaking his heart. There were times when he honestly didn't know how he could get out of bed and face the day. There were other times when he was so angry at what had happened he thought he'd like to see her dead, but he knew he could never do anything to hurt Renee. The fact was, in spite of his newly professed hatred of her, he still loved her.

While he didn't like politics, and stayed as far away from it as he could, he was following the election contest between Bob Salazar and Reverend Jacobs with a great deal of interest. He'd even given Reverend Jacobs a large political contribution, financially footing an expensive mailer that gave all the reasons why Reverend Jacobs would make a very good county supervisor and why Bob Salazar would make a very bad one. Mitch had a number of employees on his ranch who were Mexican and even though the reverend's inner circle had asked Mitch to make a big deal of Bob being Mexican, he stopped short of doing that, because he was afraid it would create problems between him and the workers on his ranch.

Mitch assumed that the mailer he'd underwritten was the reason why Bob had dropped out of the race a few days after it was delivered to voters in the county. He felt good that he'd had a part in defeating Salazar. The morning after the election he poured himself a cup of coffee and opened the paper to see what the reverend's final vote count was, so he could call him and congratulate him on his win. It wasn't to be.

The large headline jumped out at him: "Salazar Wins County Supervisor's Seat by a Landslide." Mitch had to read it three times before he fully comprehended what it meant. He took a sip of his coffee and sat back wondering what had happened that would cause this bizarre election result. After all, Bob Salazar had publicly dropped out of the race and by all rights should not have won the election, but he had. The newspaper recounted a number of theories, but no one could actually explain why it had happened. That was between each individual voter and their ballot and neither one of them was talking.

He spent the next few weeks deeply depressed. Even the pills couldn't pull him out of it. Everyone knew Renee had left him for Bob Salazar and then to have Bob win the county supervisor's seat after he'd dropped out of the election was almost too much for Mitch to bear. He became consumed with how he could get back at Renee and Bob for ruining his life. One day he saw a photograph in the paper of Bob, Renee, her sister Laura, and their new baby, Celia. The article stated that Laura, a nurse, had agreed to live with the Salazars so Renee could continue to have her psychology practice and be an active and supportive political wife.

Mitch had met Laura on a number of previous occasions, and slowly a plan began to form in his mind - a way of getting back at Renee, yet one that would not cause any harm to her. He thought about his plan for several days before deciding it was very, very workable. While Laura's death would cause considerable psychological harm to Renee, it would not physically harm her, but was a way to get back at her for what she had done to him.

He bided his time, waiting for the perfect time and place to carry out his plan. When he read in the local paper that the new county supervisor and his wife would be attending the wedding and reception of a friend, he knew he'd found the right venue. The article had even stated it would provide a much need afternoon and night out for the couple – a time when they would simply be wishing Bob's friend, Roger Langley, and his bride, Liz Lucas, congratulations. The article had gone on to state that Renee's sister, Laura Hutchison, would be helping them by taking care of their infant daughter at Cindy's Bed & Breakfast in Red Cedar.

Mitch went into the den and unlocked his gun cabinet. He took the .38 caliber pistol equipped with a long cylindrical silencer from its case and looked at it. His father had used the pistol many years earlier to hunt varmints at night on the ranch. He'd attached a silencer to the end of the gun barrel so there would be no sound of a gunshot which could frighten the cattle and cause a stampede. *Yes*, he thought, *this could easily handle the job, and it's been in the family so long there's no way it could be traced to me.*

CHAPTER THIRTEEN

"Bob, it's Roger. Were you and Renee able to get any sleep last night?"

"Yes, but it was a very long night. Renee had to break the news to her mother, and Camille did not take it well. We're headed there shortly. We're going to take her to our house for a while. She's volunteered to help out with Celia, so Renee can go back to her psychology practice, but I think that will be a week or two. I don't know what we'll do then. The more we think about what happened to Laura, the more senseless it becomes."

"I agree. It's completely senseless. Have you heard from Wes, the coroner, or Seth, the police chief?"

"Yes and no. The coroner called this morning and told me he wouldn't be able to do an autopsy until tomorrow afternoon. He said a very preliminary examination indicated Laura was shot at close range by a .38 caliber pistol. I haven't heard from the police chief."

"Well, that's no surprise. I'd be willing to bet Seth is already at Gertie's Diner telling anyone who will listen all about the crime. I also wouldn't be surprised to see it in the paper tomorrow morning. It was probably too late to get it in this morning's edition, or at least I didn't see it if it was."

"Roger, I can't even begin to tell you how many calls I've had from people who heard about it and want to help. I finally quit answering my phone, and I'm letting the calls go to my answerphone. Everyone from the mail boy at the supervisor's office to the mail girl at the law firm in San Francisco has called, not to mention our friends and people associated with Renee's practice. It's really quite overwhelming to both of us."

"I'm sure it is, but it's not surprising. You must be well-liked by the local residents of the county to win by such a wide margin. You know, Bob, I never asked you what made you change your mind about taking the job of county supervisor even though you'd withdrawn from the race."

There was a long uncomfortable silence on the other end of the phone. Roger finally broke it and said, "Bob, my legal training is telling me you're withholding something from me. If I'm going to help you, you've got to tell me everything that's relevant to the case. Something else we've never discussed is whether or not there's someone, say a former lover, who would like to get back at you for marrying Renee."

Again Bob was silent. Then he began to speak in a slow deliberate tone of voice. "Roger, is there any chance you could meet me late this afternoon at my law office? I'm still making the transition to county supervisor which is a full time job, so I'm leaving my law office open for a couple of months while I complete working on some pending cases. At the moment, the learning curve is high for my new job as county supervisor, but there are some cases in my law office that I need to make sure are handled properly. Let's meet at five. I'd rather tell you about a few things that might be of interest to you in person rather than on the phone."

"Yes, that would be fine. I'll see you then and again, please tell Renee how sorry I am about this."

"Actually, I think Renee is talking to Liz right now. I heard her say she was glad to hear from Liz."

"I'm not surprised. Liz and I talked last night and made some notes on what each of us thought needed to be done, and we kind of assigned the tasks. I'm glad to hear Liz is already on this."

"So am I, but I think it's too bad the two of you are spending your honeymoon trying to find out who killed Laura. At least Renee and I had a real honeymoon."

"You may have had the honeymoon," Roger said, "but I sure wouldn't want to go through what you you're going through. I'm okay not having a honeymoon if it means we don't have to go through something like that. See you at 5:00."

*****

When Renee answered the phone, Liz said, "Renee, I'm so sorry to bother you, but Roger and I were talking about Laura's case last night, and we made some notes. There are a couple of things I would like to follow up on. First of all, I think I know the director of the center where her ex-husband was receiving treatment, but I want to make sure before I contact him. I thought you said it was the Serenity Center."

"Yes. That's where he was. Are you familiar with it?"

"Not as to the program itself, but I've met the director at a couple of civic events. Actually, he even bought some gift cards from the spa for treatments and gave them to his staff last Christmas. As I remember, he was very nice."

"I think Serenity Center is one of the best ones around. Over the years I've worked closely with the director, Mike Hadley. He does a really good job. The Center has one of the lowest rates of recidivism - the rate of people who go back to drugs. When Laura told me Nick was going to try to get off of them for good after they were divorced, I recommended the Center to her. When you contact Mike, feel free to use my name."

"Will do. The second thing I'd like from you is the name of the wealthy rancher you were engaged to. I'm sure he had nothing to do with it, but I'd like to find out what I can about him."

"Even though I didn't marry him, Mitch Warren is one of the nicest people I've ever met."

"I'm sure he is, Renee, and I find it hard to believe he'd do anything that would hurt you, but since you did spurn him, he certainly qualifies as a possible suspect, in other words, someone who might have a reason for wanting to see you hurt."

She sighed softly into the phone. "Believe me, if there had been any way I could have gotten out of that relationship without hurting Mitch, I would have. I know I hurt him deeply, and I'll always regret that, but once I met Bob there was no one else for me, certainly not Mitch. I know he didn't understand why I couldn't marry him after so many years, but Bob became my life, and I've never regretted marrying him."

"I understand, and it's obvious he's crazy about you."

"Liz, there's someone else I hurt when I became involved with Bob - my father. I loved him dearly, but I couldn't make him see what a wonderful man Bob is. He refused to give me away or even attend my wedding. All my father saw was that Bob was a Mexican, and my father was one of those who strongly believed they should all be sent back to Mexico. He couldn't believe his daughter would marry one. When I was pregnant with Celia, who my father said he never wanted to see, he found out Laura was going to be our nurse and live with us, which only further infuriated him."

"I can only imagine how hurt you must have been. Had you been close to him prior to your relationship with Bob?"

"Very. He and my mother divorced when I was quite young, but I have to give both of them credit. They never bad-mouthed the other one to either Laura or me."

"Did either of them remarry?" Liz asked.

"Yes, my father did. My stepmother worshiped the ground he walked on. She was actually pretty obsessed with him. He literally could do no wrong in her eyes. She and I got along very well until I developed a relationship with Bob, and then she turned into a block of ice. If my father believed in something, Nancy believed in the same thing. In all the time I've known her, I honestly don't think she's ever had an opinion of her own. Every opinion she had was the opinion my father held, and when my father and I became estranged, Nancy and I became estranged. Simple as that. I was no longer in either of their lives, and she did the same thing to Laura. Seems like such a waste."

"Renee, I don't mean to be grilling you, but I do have one last question, and again, I have no idea what any of this means, but we have to start somewhere."

"I understand. What can I answer for you?"

"Roger mentioned that Bob dropped out of the race for county supervisor about two weeks before the election. He gave the reason that he wanted to spend more time with you and Celia. Do you know why he made that decision? Roger told me he'd been very active in county politics. I understand that's how the two of you met. Is there something I should know about that?"

Renee was quiet for some time. "Liz, I've often wondered about why he dropped out of the race. He never asked my opinion or gave me any reason other than what you just said. He left one morning telling me he was cautiously optimistic about winning the race and came home that evening and told me he'd held a press conference and dropped out of the race, giving me the reason you just mentioned. I wish I could tell you more. I just don't know."

"Thank you, Renee. Again, I want to tell you how sorry Roger and I are about Laura. If there's anything you need, or if I can help in any way, please call me. Oh, by the way, I just had a thought. I've never heard Bob mention his parents. Are they still alive?"

"Yes, they live in the Central Valley. I've only met them once. We had a very small wedding, and they were in the middle of a harvest and couldn't make it. Actually, none of his family was there, and since Bob was persona non grata with my father, Laura and my mother were the only ones on my side of the family."

"Can you tell me a little about Bob's parents? Seems like they'd be pretty proud of their son."

"Like I said, I've only met them once. We drove down to their house in the Central Valley. They have a lot of farm land there. Although Bob told me their land is quite valuable, their home was very small. Bob said they'd lived in it as long as he could remember. He was the youngest of six children and pretty much the only one who had made something of himself. I guess two of his sisters had children out of wedlock, and all three of his brothers were involved in drugs. They worked on the family farm for a while, but two were killed in drug deals that went bad, and the third's in prison for dealing drugs. His two sisters live at home with his parents, and his mother is helping to raise their children. Although he didn't have many good things to say about his sisters or his brothers, he's clearly devoted to his parents."

"In that case it seems very strange to me they wouldn't have come to your wedding. Were they at the swearing-in ceremony when Bob became a county supervisor following the election?"

"No. I remember asking him at the time if they didn't like me. I think I said something like 'maybe they don't approve of our marriage, because I'm twenty years younger than you are.' He told me that had nothing to do with it. He said at their age they preferred to stay home and take care of the farm. It seemed a little odd to me, but maybe it's the truth. I don't know, and I certainly wouldn't feel comfortable asking his sisters. I don't think they're dealing drugs, but I sure wouldn't be surprised if they were using them. It's pretty sad when you think about it."

"I couldn't agree more. Is there anything I can do for you?"

"The best thing you could do for me is find out who killed Laura.

I know that guests are supposed to give a newlywed couple like you and Roger a present, but in this case, if you could find out who killed Laura, you'd be giving me the best present I could ever have."

After ending her phone call with Renee, Liz spent the rest of the morning and early afternoon with Roger and their four children, Jonah, Brittany, Cole, and Jake. Cole was taking the other three to the San Francisco airport so they could catch their various flights that afternoon and early evening.

Hugs, kisses, and best wishes abounded. Finally, all four doors were closed on Cole's car, and everyone waved as the car made its way down the lane to the highway that led to San Francisco.

When the car could no longer be seen, Roger put his arms around Liz and said, "Well, I've said it before, it's just us now, you and me in our new life." Winston barked as if to say, *wrong! I'm here and I'm part of this new life you're talking about.* He tried to slip between the two of them, but Roger was holding Liz as close as he could, and Winston couldn't squeeze in. He looked forlornly up at Roger, not sure what his role was going to be with this new relationship.

CHAPTER FOURTEEN

When Roger walked into Bob's law office that afternoon at five o'clock, Bob said, "You're prompt Roger, but you always were. Come on in. I've got a secretary, but she only works here in the mornings. She's really good, and I wanted to take her with me, so she's at my supervisor's office in the afternoons. Have a seat, and let's get started. Renee's doing better, but I don't want to leave her alone for long, although now that her mother's with her, I think it will help. The downside is that her mother is grieving as much as Renee, although Renee also has a huge sense of guilt. She feels if we hadn't hired Laura to take care of Celia, she'd still be alive." He shrugged his shoulders. "She might be right."

"As I mentioned to you on the phone this morning, Bob, I'm very curious why you decided to drop out of the supervisor's race with only a couple of weeks to go given your interest in politics and the fact that you were kind of the fair-haired boy. I know you hate to hear it, but I think it's safe to say you were also the Republican's token Mexican. Can you tell me why you dropped out?"

Bob stood up, walked over to the window, and stood looking out of it for several long moments. Finally he started speaking to Roger, and from the tone of his voice Roger could tell this was a very painful subject for him to talk about.

"I received an anonymous phone call in the early afternoon of the day I dropped out of the race. The person told me he was sending a courier over to my office that would be there momentarily with proof that my parents were illegal immigrants, and he would make sure they were exposed and sent back to Mexico. The courier came with a manila envelope while I was on the phone with the caller. My secretary signed for it and brought it to me.

"The man on the phone told me to open the envelope and look at the contents. He had solid documentation that my parents were illegals along with their photographs, photos of their farm, and a lot of other personal information about my family and parents. He told me if I didn't drop out of the race that very day, there would be an expose of the information in the papers the next morning about my parents as well as negative information about my brothers and sisters."

"Bob, let me interrupt. From what you're saying, I'm assuming that your parents are illegal immigrants. Is that true?"

"Yes. Over the years I tried to get them to become American citizens, particularly when I became involved in politics. I know people, and there are ways those things can be expedited. Unfortunately, I never could convince my parents to do it. They were sure they'd be sent back to Mexico. That was the excuse they used. Between you and me, I think they were afraid that everyone would know about my brothers and sisters. I'm almost certain they wouldn't do it because of that."

"Do you think your parents would have been sent back to Mexico?"

"If they'd done it the way I wanted them to I could have guaranteed them they wouldn't be sent to Mexico. The anonymous caller told me he had people who would gladly make sure they were sent back to Mexico when they were exposed as being in the country illegally. Roger, I couldn't risk that. My parents supported and encouraged me from the time I was a little boy to make more of my life than they had. I know I wouldn't be where I am today if it hadn't been for them. I could not and would not allow myself to be the cause of their being deported. It's as simple as that. I called a press conference late that afternoon and dropped out of the race."

"How did Renee feel about it?"

"As much as it pained me and as close as we are, I didn't tell her. I knew she'd urge me to continue on with the race. She probably would have told me my parents would want me to stay in the race and not want to stand in the way of my becoming an important political figure in the state."

"That had to be a very tough decision you had to make, Bob. I admire you for doing it. What did you think when the numbers came in on election night, and you learned you won by a landslide?"

"Quite frankly, I couldn't believe it. The numbers were far greater than the campaign consultants I'd hired before I dropped out had predicted. Let me answer the next question I'm sure you're going to ask. You want to know why I decided to accept the position even though I'd dropped out of the race."

"Yes, that's exactly where I was headed. Why did you do it?"

"I'm kind of an old-fashioned politician. I never got into politics to feed my ego. I really want to help people, and I particularly want to help my fellow Mexicans. I decided if there was that much of an overwhelming mandate for me to become a county supervisor, then I would bow to the will of the people and accept the position. I felt I owed it to the people who had both supported me and voted for me."

"Have to ask you again, Bob, what did Renee think of your decision?"

"She's such a wonderful understanding woman. I told her just what I told you about the will of the people of Dillon County. I didn't hear anything more from the anonymous caller, and I assumed that with my win and my acceptance of the seat there would be no more threats against my parents. After all, I'd done what the caller had demanded by dropping out of the race."

"So you think there's a good chance that Laura's murder was politically motivated?"

"Of course, wouldn't you?"

"Yes, I probably would. We both know your expertise in law is in estate planning and taxes, and as you know, mine's in criminal law. I always look to see who has the most to gain when a crime is committed. In your case, regarding the phone call, it would have been your opponent, the Reverend Lou Jacobs, who had the most to gain. Do you think he was behind it?"

"You can't even begin to imagine how many times I've asked myself that very question. Yes, he could have been behind it, but he wasn't the one on the phone. I'm certain of that. But Roger, here's the thing I keep struggling with. What does this have to do with Laura's death? I can't believe the reverend, a man of God, would have anything to do with her death. I heard he was furious that I'd won, and he'd lost again, but I just can't see him hiring someone to kill her, so he could, in some strange way, retaliate against me."

"Bob, you're a smart man. All you need to do is take a look at history and see how many wars were fought in the name of religion. And I hate to play the race card, but it's well-known that the reverend's church caters to the most conservative of the conservatives. Don't think a lot of those people would be real happy about having a Mexican represent them."

"Yes, I suppose there is some truth to that. The problem is it could be anyone associated with the reverend or his church. If it's someone he knows, they could have murdered Laura as a vendetta against me, but there's a good chance the reverend knows nothing about it. As a matter of fact, I had a very nice voicemail from him today expressing his condolences. He said something about although we've certainly had our differences, he wouldn't wish these circumstances on anyone. I thought that was a nice gesture."

"That may be all it is, Bob, a nice gesture attempting to divert your thinking. I know I sound very cold-hearted, but in my practice I've come to learn that most unsavory people don't usually decide to do good things out of the kindness of their hearts. Anyway, I want to switch to another topic. When I was on the phone with you this morning I asked you about relationships you had prior to Renee."

"Roger, I don't think that's very important. Sure, there were a few, but they were kind of meaningless."

"You may have considered them meaningless, but that doesn't mean they weren't meaningful to someone else. Who comes to mind?"

Bob took a deep breath and avoided looking directly at Roger.

CHAPTER FIFTEEN

Bob sat at his desk, the index fingers on his hands steepled with his forehead resting on them. He took a deep breath. "Roger, you have to believe me when I tell you that Candy really meant nothing to me. You're a man of the world. Sometimes a man gets caught up by a woman, and she holds him in her net, refusing to release him."

"Am I to understand that Candy was one of those women?"

"Yes." He looked at Bob and said, "I met Candy when I was working in San Francisco. I went to a bar after work one night, and she was there with friends. There was an instant attraction, and from that time on we saw each other a couple of times a week until I moved to Dillon and met Renee."

"Bob, I think you can do a little better with the description of the relationship than what you've told me. Try again, and I especially need to know more about Candy. Please, don't hold back. It's just too important for you to do that."

He stood up and began pacing the floor. "Candy was from an Italian family that owned a couple of restaurants located on one of the piers in San Francisco. She was the stereotypical Italian woman, a dark-haired passionate beauty with a temper to match. Even though I'm no longer tangled up in her net, I have to say she was a fascinating woman."

"How did you end the relationship?" Roger asked.

"The same way it started. Even though I'd moved to the city of Dillon and opened my law practice there, I had to go back to San Francisco now and then to take care of some loose ends. I'd met Renee and knew that I wanted her to be my wife. You see, there was a big difference between the two women. I loved Renee, and I was infatuated with Candy. Unfortunately, Candy didn't understand the difference. When we met for drinks that night, I told her I thought she was one of the most fascinating women I'd ever met, but I had found someone else I wanted to spend my life with. You can imagine how well that went over."

"What did she say?"

"You have to understand the background of her family. These were hot-blooded Italians who were very well-known in San Francisco. They were used to taking whatever they wanted from their restaurants on the pier to buying politicians to do their bidding. Losing was not an option for them, and that's exactly what Candy told me. Her brothers were involved in some things I always thought it was better that I not know about. Candy told me they had told her they would have preferred that she find an Italian rather than a Mexican, but at least I was someone they wouldn't have to be embarrassed about. She told me they'd be furious when they learned I had broken up with her."

"Was she emotional about it when you told her?"

"That might be the understatement of the year. I remember trying to quiet her down, because she was screaming so loudly that everyone in the cocktail lounge had stopped talking and was listening to her. It was not my finest moment."

"I can well imagine. How did it end?"

"Not well. I realized she was never going to understand why I preferred someone else to her, so I got up, put some money on the table, and told her goodbye. That was pretty much it." He stopped talking, looked down, and twisted his wedding ring around his finger.

"Bob, I hope you understand that I'm not trying to push you, but if I'm going to help you, I need to know everything, and I have a feeling you're deliberately leaving something out."

"Yeah, and I suppose that's what makes you such a good lawyer. Well, I might as well tell you. The last words Candy screamed at me were 'You better watch your back, and whoever the woman is who stole you from me better watch hers as well.' At the time I didn't think much of it, figuring it was just a passionate outburst. Those words have been haunting me ever since Laura was murdered. I know Candy would never commit murder, but her brothers had a number of associates who were clearly capable of it and more than willing to do it in order to please them."

"Do you know what's happened to her? Has she found someone else? If she's happily married to some Italian guy that the family loves, maybe that's all it was - words uttered in a passionate moment."

"No, I haven't seen her or talked to her since that night. I have no idea where she is or who she's with."

"You may remember that the law firm has a great investigator I've used over the years by the name of Sean. I'll give him a call and see what he can find out. When he's finished we'll know everything about her from the moment you stopped seeing her to the moment he stops investigating her. By the way, what's her last name? Sean will need that."

"Poncinello."

"Are you kidding me? Bob, everyone in San Francisco knows that name. It's rather infamous. You certainly picked someone with a checkered family past. As I recall, there was some scandal years ago about a Mafia murder taking place at one of their restaurants. No one was ever arrested and the scandal died a natural death. I guess you're right, with the kind of money I've read they spend on supporting politicians they can pretty much do whatever they want. Is there anything else I should know? And does Renee know anything about Candy?"

"Renee knows I was seeing someone in San Francisco, and I ended it when I fell in love with her. Beyond that, there was no reason for her to know. Think about it Roger, I was forty-eight when I fell in love with Renee. She was twenty-eight. Neither of us were children. I know she was engaged to a rancher, Mitch Warren, when we met, and she knew I'd had a number of relationships over the years. At my age, you're going to bring a little baggage to the church on your wedding day. As much in love as we were and still are, neither one of us cared about the other's past relationships. It simply wasn't important."

"Yes, I understand."

Bob looked at Roger intently. "Roger, I know Renee feels she might have been the cause of Laura's death, but I'm concerned it might have been because of me, not her, that Laura was killed. It very easily could have been a political vendetta or, on the other hand, it could have had something to do with my spurning Candy. In both of those situations, I could be the cause of Laura's death. If I was, I'm not sure I'll ever be able to forgive myself, and I don't know if Renee will be able to forgive me. Please help me."

"I'll do everything I can. I know it sounds simplistic, but try not to worry. Renee and Celia really need you now. You have to be there for them. I'll let you know the minute I find something out."

"Roger, thanks. I feel better knowing you're looking into it. From what you told me about the local police chief, Seth Williams, it doesn't sound like he'd ever be able to find out who did it."

"Bob, much as I hate to admit it, Liz is probably better at this than I am. She's solved several other murders, including one that took place in one of her cottages out at the spa. Then there was the murder of a young man who was interning for her in the kitchen of the lodge, and the last one she solved was the murder of Seth's deputy. I gave her advice, but she was the one who solved the cases. So look at it this way. You're getting two sleuths for the price of one. I may have a few credentials after my name, but Liz has the nose of a bloodhound. She calls it her niggle." He put his hand out to shake Bob's. "I'll be talking to you soon."

CHAPTER SIXTEEN

Roger could smell the garlic before he even opened the door to the lodge. "What are you fixing for dinner? It smells wonderful, but before you tell me, first I need a hug and a kiss from my wife," he said taking Liz in his arms. Winston stood next to her and looked up at Roger. He'd learned it was probably a good thing if he didn't try to get between them when they were doing whatever it was humans did when they stood close together like they were right now.

After a moment, Liz stepped back and looked up at Roger. "I figured we both needed some comfort food after the events of last night. We're having a mixture of mussels, clams, and shrimp in an herb broth served in a big bowl along with a crusty loaf of sourdough bread and a mixed green salad with a light vinaigrette dressing? How does that sound?"

"Absolutely fabulous. If I was in a restaurant that's probably what I'd order, plus it looks like it's going to rain. I think I'll start a fire, and we'll curl up on the couch for the evening, but first I'll open that bottle of sauvignon blanc I saw in the refrigerator this morning. That should be perfect with the meal. Okay with you?"

"Sounds great. I've prepped dinner as much as I can, and I'd really like to hear what Bob told you, plus I learned some interesting things from Renee that I'm going to follow up on tomorrow. You want to go first or do you want me to?"

He handed her a glass of the chilled wine and said, "Here's what I found out from Bob." He spent the next half hour telling her about Bob's relationship with Candy and the anonymous phone call Bob had received.

"Well, given what he told you I can understand why he dropped out of the race," Liz said, "but it sure is ironic he won. I'd hate to think Reverend Jacobs was behind Laura's murder, however, it's certainly a possibility. He's a three time political loser, and this time he lost to a Mexican. It had to be a humiliating defeat for him. He's made it very clear what his position is on the illegal immigrant issue as well as the Mexicans. I read one time where he even said they were all rapists and belonged in jail. He has a large following, so a lot of people must agree with what he's putting out there, and based on that, it very well could have been one of his followers who committed the crime. If it was one of his followers it's going to be very difficult to find out who it was."

"I know. I need to call Sean and see what he can find out about the reverend. I also want him to do some research on Bob's ex-girlfriend. I'll call him now, and he may be able to get something for me tonight or early tomorrow morning."

"Roger, would you ask him if he can find out anything about the wealthy rancher Renee was engaged to? His name is Mitch Warren. I was actually going to tell you about him and see if it was okay if I called Sean."

"Sure. Let me call him now and get that out of the way." He picked up his cell phone and punched in Sean's number. "Sean, it's Roger. Sorry to bother you after hours, but I've got a little research I'd like you to take care of when you have time." He listened to Sean for a moment. "Perfect, glad you have some time tonight. Here's what I need. I want everything you can get on a reverend in Dillon, California, named Lou Jacobs." He listened a minute. "Yeah, that's right. He lives in the city of Dillon. There's also the county of Dillon. That's where he ran for Dillon County Supervisor and lost. Anyway, he's got a big charismatic church there. Remember Bob Salazar? He used to work for our law firm, and he's the one who beat Reverend

Jacobs in the election.

"The next person I'd like to know about is a wealthy rancher in the area by the name of Mitch Warren. Lastly, there's a family in San Francisco, name of Poncinello..."

Liz heard Sean's voice coming through the phone. "Poncinello? Are you sure? That's a family you really don't want to mess around with. They've never even been arrested because every law enforcement person and politician in San Francisco is in their pocket, plus we're talking about people who have no sense of morals. They mess up businesses and make people disappear before they've even had breakfast. The day just gets worse after that. Are you sure you want to open that can of worms?"

Roger sighed. "I wish it wasn't necessary, but yes, I do need to know about them. I'm particularly interested in one of their daughters, a woman by the name of Candy Poncinello. See what you can come up with on her and Sean, thanks. I'm sure there are a lot of other things you could be doing tonight." He ended the call.

"What was that about some woman named Candy?" Liz asked.

Roger told her about Bob's relationship with her and her parting words to him.

"Wow! Did you know he was having an affair with some hot-blooded Italian?"

"No. Bob is a very discreet man. I never met any of the women he was involved with, and from what he told me today, I guess there have been a few."

"I'm not surprised. He's a very attractive man. I would expect him to have had a number of relationships with women, plus he's our age, and he's never been married. It's not too much of a stretch to think of a number of women who would be interested in a handsome Latino. Bob has what I call 'dancing eyes,' and I think that's one of the reasons he's so attractive. They say the eyes are the windows to a person's soul, and if that's true, he's got a smiling soul."

"Sorry, Liz, I have a little problem with Bob having a smiling soul. He may have other positive assets, but come on, a smiling soul? There's something else that kind of bothers me about this man you refer to as having a smiling soul. Let me tell you why he dropped out of the race, and then I'd like to hear your thoughts."

When he'd finished telling her, Liz said, "I can totally understand why he didn't want his parents to be hurt because of him, but I'm getting a little concerned about a pattern I'm seeing. From what you've said, he never told Renee about Candy, only that he had been seeing someone, but it sounds like a little more than that. Secondly, why didn't he tell Renee about the phone call? Doesn't seem like he's being very straightforward with her, and I don't think it's very good to withhold things like that in a relationship, particularly when you're married, which makes me think, Mr. Langley, is there something I should know about you that you haven't told me?"

"Fraid not, sweetheart. What you see is what you got. You know I was married. You know my wife died from cancer, and you know that you were the first woman I started seeing after her. Not much of a story there."

"I'll take your word for it, but I have to tell you it does make me feel better, anyway, back to Bob and Renee. I had a long conversation with her this morning. Here's what I found out." She told him about Renee's long-time relationship with Mitch Warren and how close he was to her father as well as the breakdown of her relationship with her father due to her involvement with Bob.

"Roger, I think we have multiple suspects here, but I'm getting the sense the killer could be someone trying to get back at Renee or Bob, rather than someone hating Laura. The only one who might hate Laura would be her ex-husband, and we don't even know if he was in or out of the Serenity Center when she was killed. What we do know is that there were a couple of people who felt they had reason to want to harm either Bob or Renee, and maybe Laura was simply the means to the end.

"Looks like the reverend or any one of his supporters or church members might have hated Bob enough to want to kill him for getting elected and beating the reverend out of the seat he'd tried for several times. Then again maybe Mitch Warren snapped when Renee told him she was going to marry Bob after their very long relationship. We should know something about each of those possibilities after Sean does some research, but I'm having a niggle about something else."

"A year ago I would have laughed if anyone had told me they had a niggle about something, but after your niggle helped solve the last couple of cases, I'm not laughing. What's your niggle?" he asked.

"Renee told me how close she and her father remained even after her parents were divorced. It's somewhat unusual that a daughter would be very close to both of her parents after their divorce, particularly given the fact that her father has been remarried for years. From what Renee told me, her stepmother idolized her father, and when he decided he would have nothing more to do with Renee, she followed his lead and did the same. When Laura told their father that she was going to live with Bob and Renee and take care of their newborn, Renee's father became estranged from Laura as well and because of Bob's Mexican heritage, refused to even see his granddaughter. I have no idea why I have a niggle, but it's enough I'd like to see what I can find out about her father and stepmother. Think I'll pay her a visit tomorrow."

"I agree that it's unusual. I know parents often don't approve of a child's spouse, but usually they reconcile. If you have a niggle, go for it, but I do have a request. I know I sound like some recording, but there has been a murder, and people will soon know that you're sleuthing again. Actually, I'm sure the police chief has already told all of the customers at Gertie's about it. Anyway, I want you to carry the gun you have, and I want Winston to be with you wherever you go. I won't try and stop you from doing this, plus I have to say you're pretty good at it, but please be careful. Remember, you're a married woman now, and I sure as heck don't want to go through the death of another wife. Understand?" he asked, giving her the most solemn look he could muster.

"Roger, I promise I'll take Winston and my gun with me. You just mentioned Gertie's, and I think it might be a good thing if we go to breakfast there tomorrow morning. That woman knows more about what's happening in this area than anyone else. Gertie's Diner is simply the gossip hub of Red Cedar and Dillon County. Now, I need to get dinner ready. You've got a few minutes. Might want to turn on the news and see if they've made Laura's murder the lead story of the night. For Bob and Renee's sake, I hope not, however, with Bob's new position, it very well might be."

"I hope not too," Roger said as he picked up the remote and turned on the television.

CHAPTER SEVENTEEN

"Liz, that was fabulous. You can fix that for me anytime. Mussels, clams, and shrimp in a white wine broth with garlic, herbs, and parsley. Plenty of bread for dunking and a salad to balance the taste. What's not to like about that?" Roger asked rubbing his stomach. "I'm stuffed. I probably should run back and forth to the highway several times to run it off, but I don't think that's going to happen."

He was interrupted by the sound of the song, "I Left My Heart in San Francisco," coming from his cell phone. He walked over to the desk where he'd left it when he finished talking to Sean earlier in the evening.

"Sean, that was fast. You really are a miracle man. What did you find out?" He listened to Sean for a moment. "Let me put you on speaker phone. I'd like Liz to hear what you have to say. Like it or not, she's already involved in this thing." Roger laughed at what Sean was saying. "No, Sean, even though we're married, I still don't have any control over what she does. Okay, shoot."

"The first one I investigated was Mitch Warren. Looks like he really had it bad for Renee. According to the records, his family convinced him to enter a private mental care facility for severe depression. Evidently he was broken-hearted after Renee left him for Bob. He was in the facility for six months. From what I learned he's never gotten back to normal. He takes a number of medications for depression..."

"Wait a minute," Roger said. "That's very privileged information. How did you find that out? Think it goes against the HIPAA privacy code."

"Boss, one of the things I never do is divulge my sources. You know that. Can't tell you. Anyway the guy lives in a world of hurt. Something interesting I found out is that he had a frequent visitor to the facility, and it was Renee's father. I managed to have a little talk with one of the women who works at the facility, and she told me she would often hear the two of them talking about a no-good Mexican by the name of Bob. She never did hear them mention a last name, but I'm making a calculated guess that it was Bob Salazar, Renee's husband. There's something more you should know. The woman told me that one time she was folding some laundry, and there was a partition between her and where Mitch and Renee's father were talking. Renee's father said something to the effect that if Mitch wanted to do something to Bob, he'd never tell anyone."

"That doesn't sound good. If this guy is still mentally off, and from what you're telling me, he seems to be, he very well might have killed Laura to get back at Bob. Maybe he felt killing Laura rather than Bob would be a lot easier, and it would definitely hurt both Renee and Bob."

"Don't know. That's one down. You asked about the Reverend Lou Jacobs. This guy's as oily as they come. He's originally from Kentucky. He attended a seminary school there and became a minister. Had a little problem with the father of one of the girls in his congregation. Seems like he caught the reverend and his underage daughter in a very compromising situation in the rectory. When the girl's father told him he was going to expose the reverend unless he left town that night, the reverend left. He came to California and settled in Dillon. From everything I learned, the guy's so smooth he could sell snake oil to someone who lives in fear of snakes. He's a real fire and brimstone preacher, and his congregation loves him. He caters to people who are completely obsessed with anti-immigration, and almost every Sunday he preaches about how the Mexicans are responsible for California's budgetary problems, the broken educational system, the overflowing prisons, and the upsurge in crime."

"Were you able to find out if he has an inner circle? Anyone claim to hear him make threats against Bob? And a thought just occurred to me. Does he lead Bible Study groups? What's his interaction with his parishioners?"

"First of all, he has a number of advisors, political and spiritual, but I don't think there's much there. As cagey as this guy is, if he wanted to get rid of someone he'd hire an outside thug. I think he's too smart to get caught with his hand in the cookie jar, so to speak. As far as interaction with his parishioners, he leads a weekly Bible Study group himself. Matter of fact, it's tomorrow night at his church."

"What about Bob's ex-girlfriend, Candy Poncinello?"

"Actually, I'm a big fan of Bob's, but don't think getting into that relationship was one of his smartest moves. I've done a little work in the past which involved that family, and they're just as dirty now as they were then. There is no doubt in my mind that if they wanted to do something to Bob or one of his loved ones, they definitely have the muscle to do it. They have connections all over the San Francisco area, many of them semi-legit or non-legit. However, based on what I found out, unless some family member kept a vendetta going against Bob for breaking up with Candy, I'd put them on the lower tier of suspects and here's why."

He went on to tell Roger that shortly after Bob broke up with Candy, one of her brothers introduced Candy to a good friend of his, the son of a well-known Italian family from Chicago who was visiting San Francisco. They married a few months later and had twin sons within the year. According to what Sean found out, they were very happy, and Candy's brothers were very proud uncles. In the research Sean had done on Candy, there was no mention of Bob Salazar.

"Thanks, Sean. As usual, you've done a superb job. When you're up for a performance review, let me know, and I'll throw in my two cents worth. It's late, and I'm sure you need to get some sleep. Again, thanks." He ended the call and turned to Liz. "Well, what do you think?"

"I think one of us needs to attend that Bible Study group that's going to be held tomorrow night. Secondly, I wonder who's running the Warren Ranch if Mitch is as depressed as Sean indicated. It doesn't sound like he'd be able to function very effectively. There must be some sort of ranch headquarters or main office in or near Dillon. Let's divide this up. Why don't you look into Mitch Warren and also attend the meeting of the Bible Study group tomorrow night? I'll check out Serenity Center, and as I've mentioned, I've got a niggle about Renee's stepmother. I'd like to see what I can find out about her. Will that work?"

"It does, and I'll be sure and let Bob know that attending a Bible Study group led by a minister who was caught in an indecent act with a minor in Kentucky and is as glib as a snake oil salesman is not my idea of how I was planning on spending my honeymoon." He sighed and said, "At least promise me we can still go to Gertie's, and I can get sausage gravy and biscuits for breakfast."

"I promise, but do I need to remind you that when you finished dinner not all that long ago you told me you probably wouldn't need to eat for a week because you were so full?"

"That was before I thought about Gertie and her sausage gravy and biscuits. I won't eat for a week after I have the sausage gravy and biscuits."

"Sure you won't. Since we don't have any guests, don't think I need to fill Brandy Boy's cask tonight. Winston, come. Time for you to go outside one last time."

CHAPTER EIGHTEEN

"Well, looky what the cat drug in. If it ain't the very newlywedded Mr. and Mrs. Langley," Gertie said in a voice loud enough that all the patrons in the entire restaurant stopped talking and clapped along with Gertie. As usual, the popular diner was full of breakfast customers, the police chief already eating his customary breakfast of eggs over easy which would result in a stain on his uniform shirt, a daily occurrence of his.

"Gotta tell ya', I wouldna' missed that weddin' for nothin'. Highlight of my year. Don't get much better than one of my favorite people marryin' my new tenant. How's that new office workin' out for ya', handsome?" Gertie asked, as she blew a big bubble from her ever present wad of bubble gum and reached up and grabbed a pencil from her bottle-blond teased hair, all the while teetering on her stiletto heels.

"Glad you enjoyed it, Gertie, and I can't thank you and your staff enough for taking care of the reception. I couldn't have done it alone," Liz said. "I know most of the staff that helped you, but when you have a little time, I'd appreciate it if you could send me the names of everyone and their addresses. I want to write each of them a personal note and thank them."

"Sure 'nuf, honey. Ain't no way to start your married life out by helpin' yer friend Bob and his wife find out who killed her sister.

Darned shame it had to happen the night of yer' weddin'."

"Gertie, I never doubted that you'd know all about it. Find out from Seth?"

"Yer' kiddin', right? Seth stopped in here right after he was at Cindy's Bed & Breakfast jawin' 'bout it. Sounds like Bob had a few enemies altho' I like him. Matter of fact, even voted for him. Seems like a purty good man, and there aren't a lot of them around, jes' ask me. I married four I thought were good, but ain't doin' that no more. Waste of time and energy."

Privately Liz wondered who would want to marry a woman who was stuck in the sixties and seventies and still dressed as if time had stopped. Gertie was a legend in the town and surrounding area along with her hamburgers and chocolate malts. Tables in the popular diner were always occupied by people who had driven up from San Francisco for one of her burgers and a malt.

"So, who do ya' think done the nasty? Liz, yer' the one who's always finding the bad guy. Who's the bad guy this time? Hear it might be Renee's old boyfriend, Laura's ex, or even that smarmy minister Bob beat in the election. What's yer' take on the situation?"

"More importantly," Roger said, "I'd like to know your take. You're the one who always finds out the latest rumor. Hear anything about the murder?"

Gertie motioned for Liz to move over and sat down next to her. "Handsome, I was 'fraid ya' weren't gonna ask me. Little birdy tol' me the two of you are gonna have yer' hands full. On top of the three I mentioned, it was a pretty well-known fact that Renee's daddy hated Bob. Him bein' a Mexican and all. Personally, I couldn't run this place without 'em, but I hear he hated him. Also heard that Bob had a fling with one of them Poncinello women. Bad juju in that family. Wouldn't be surprised at anything they did, but back to Renee's daddy. I knew him purty well, and he was so proud of Renee and Laura. Never made no sense for him to turn his back on them. Sumthin' jes' don't ring true there. Been thinkin' 'bout it. Over the years her daddy came in here with his new wife from time to time."

"Gertie, his new wife wasn't exactly new. They were married for over twenty years."

"Yeah, that may be true, but she's a weird bird. Don't think she ever had an original thought in her life. She was like a little parrot, jes' parrotin' whatever Don said. Used to see her and Renee in here jawin' it up. Thought it was a real nice touch on Renee's part - ya' know, bein' the good daughter and makin' nice with her stepmom. Musta been hard, cuz I know Renee and her mother are very close. And now to have her sister murdered."

"Any other ideas, Gertie?" Roger asked.

"Well," she said, looking around to make sure no one was listening, "Sounds to me like somebody was tryin' to get back at Renee or Bob. Can't think of any reason why anyone would wanta' murder Laura. She was as sweet as they come, course there is that no-good druggie she married. Hear he's out of Serenity. Any truth to it?"

"Actually I'm going over there today and talk to the director. Renee didn't know if he'd left the Center, although he's been there three months, and that's the usual treatment time for someone who goes in voluntarily for rehab, according to Renee. I'll know more later on today. I know he's had a problem with drug abuse, but killing the woman who was his wife? I have a hard time with that."

"Yeah, so do I, but wouldn't be any more surprisin' than a man of God murderin' her or havin' her murdered. Thinkin' ya' got yer' work cut out for ya'. Enjoyed the talk. Gotta get back to work. Assume it'll be the breakfast usual, sausage gravy and biscuits. Half the people who come here in the mornin' ask for that. Purty popular. If I hear anything, I'll let ya' know."

"Gertie, there's no one I would rather hear from than you. Gertie's Diner is the hub of Red Cedar, and you're at the center of that hub. Again, thanks for your help at the reception."

"My pleasure, darlins', my pleasure." She stood up and tottered off to the kitchen to place their order. Liz looked at Roger and grinned.

"See what you have to look forward to when I'm her age?" she asked.

"Don't think so. For one thing bottle-blond is not my favorite hair color and secondly, I'd hate to see you take a fall because you insisted on wearing five inch high heels, but I will say this. There's no one quite like Gertie. She's definitely an original."

CHAPTER NINETEEN

"Roger, it's almost noon, and I probably won't be back until around dinner time. You said you had a couple of places to go as well. I'll take Winston and see you later. Who knows? Maybe one of us will get lucky this afternoon."

"For Bob and Renee's sake, I certainly hope so. Be careful. Love you."

Forty-five minutes later, Liz and Winston turned down the lane next to the large sign that read "Serenity Center." She parked her van in front of the center.

Although she'd met the director of the center, she had no idea who owned it, but from the looks of it, money was not an issue. The center was a large white building with an attractive security gate and fence surrounding it. The only thing that hinted at the nature of the center was the concertina wire which was strung on top of the fence and gate, effectively keeping the people who committed themselves to the three month program from spontaneously leaving. Between the fence and the wraparound porch was a neatly manicured lawn. Hanging baskets with bright, cheery blossoming flowers were secured by wires which had been hung from the porch roof.

Porch swings and cushioned furniture were inviting to guests and those who had chosen to deal with their addictions at Serenity

Center. Next to the welcoming front door, which had been painted red, was a neatly painted sign that read "May All Who Enter Find Peace."

Liz knocked on the door and a moment later it was opened by a large man. He looked at Liz and said, "Hi, I'm Mike Hadley. Welcome to Serenity Center. How may I help you?" He looked further at her for a moment and continued, "I'm sorry, Liz, I didn't recognize you with that big dog." He bent down and let Winston sniff his hand. Standing up he said, "I'd heard you had a guard dog at the spa, and I'm assuming this is the dog."

"Yes. This is Winston. Winston, this is Mike Hadley." Winston was sitting next to Liz and put his paw up as if to shake Mike's hand.

"How did you teach him that? We've got a dog here at the center, but trust me, getting him housebroken was about as good as it got." He shook Winston's paw. "Liz, I'm assuming this isn't a social visit. Let's go into my office." He walked down the hall and into an office with the word "Director" in brass letters on the door. "Please have a seat. Winston, you can sit next to her. What can I help you with?" Mike asked.

"Mike, I'm sure you have confidentiality issues when it comes to releasing information about someone who is or who has been at Serenity Center for drug or alcohol problems, and of course I would never ask you to violate anyone's confidence. Here's what I'm dealing with. A very good friend of my husband's..."

He held his hand up. "I'm sorry. I certainly am being remiss in not congratulating you on your recent wedding. I appreciate the invitation to your reception, but we were having an issue with a guest here at the Center, and I couldn't leave it to the staff. Please, go on."

"Bob Salazar, the new county supervisor and his wife, Renee, were at our wedding and the reception which followed. The two of them, their young daughter, and her sister, a nurse who was helping take care of their newborn daughter, were all staying at Cindy's Bed & Breakfast. Unfortunately her sister was murdered at Cindy's, and their young daughter was in the room when it happened. Cindy heard the baby crying and when it had gone on longer than she thought was normal, she went into the room and discovered that Laura Hutchinson had been murdered. The child was hysterical. Who knows what's embedded in her psyche?"

"I hadn't heard about it. I haven't been to Gertie's for a couple of days, and we've had no new guests out here, so that's not unexpected." He grinned and said, "I'm sure if I'd been at Gertie's for breakfast I probably would have heard Seth telling everyone all about it and what he was personally doing to solve it. Would I be right?" he asked, his eyes twinkling.

"Absolutely. I'm here because Laura's husband was Nick Hutchinson. I know he voluntarily checked himself into Serenity Center to deal with drug addiction. His sister-in-law, Renee, recommended the Center."

Mike snapped his fingers. "Of course, now it's all coming together. Renee's a very respected psychologist in the area. She and I have worked together from time to time with people who had addiction issues. I haven't seen her or talked to her since she and Bob got married. I know she was helping him in his campaign and was working fewer hours. I didn't know that Nick was her former brother-in-law. When you mentioned the name Laura Hutchinson it rang a bell, but I couldn't place it. Now I do. I conducted a number of group therapy sessions which Nick Hutchinson took part in, and that's where I've heard Laura's name."

"Mike, you said you conducted, as in the past tense. Does that mean Nick is no longer here at the center?"

"That's correct. He left a week ago. That's about all I can tell you."

"I understand. Let's speak generally. When someone completes a three month intensive session at the Center, is there any type of follow-up? I guess I'm asking if a former patient is assigned to a mentor or if you require them to check in with someone. I really don't know what the proscribed procedure is."

"We ask that people who complete a three month treatment check in with a sponsor or mentor here at the Center every forty-eight hours for the first month. After that it drops to once a week and eventually to once a month." He opened the bottom drawer of his desk and took out a file.

"I don't think I'm breaking any confidentiality rules by telling you that Nick Hutchinson has not checked in with his sponsor since he left a week ago. I have a note here that his sponsor is very concerned about him. He hasn't answered telephone calls and isn't at the apartment where he was formerly living." Mike looked through the file and then across the desk at Liz. "He was an exemplary guest while he was here and his sponsor said he had every reason to believe he would be able to lead a productive life free from drugs. Yesterday he put a note in Nick's file indicating that when someone did not check in with their sponsor, it was a big red flag that the person may have returned to, in Nick's case, drug use. Beyond that, I can't tell you anything. I hope it helps."

"I don't know if it helps, but at least I know he's out, and he possibly could be a suspect, not that we need another one."

"Liz, I voted for Bob Salazar, and I like him. He seems like a real straight shooter, and I was sorry when Renee started working fewer hours, and we had less interactions, because I really enjoyed working with her. Let me do this. If Nick's sponsor hears from him, I'll let you know. Beyond that there's not much I can do."

"Thanks, Mike," she said standing up and motioning to Winston. "I really appreciate what you've told me. Let me ask you one more thing. Do you have any reason to believe Nick Hutchinson could be violent? In other words, would there be any reason for him to want to harm Laura?"

Mike was quiet for several moments, deep in thought, and then he spoke. "Liz, let's speak theoretically. If one of our guests came here hoping to repair a marriage or even reconcile with someone from whom they'd become estranged, and after they'd gone through the program and that person still would have nothing to do with them, then yes, someone with a strong substance abuse problem could become violent. Since you're wondering if Nick Hutchinson was responsible for his wife's murder, I don't know. Could he or anyone else be capable of it given those circumstances? I would have to say yes. And Liz, if you hear something, would you let me know?"

"Of course, you've been more than generous with your time and your information. Winston, come." When she and Winston were in the van she looked back at the center and saw Mike in the doorway. She smiled and waved to him, as she and Winston drove back down the lane.

CHAPTER TWENTY

Liz had gotten the address of Renee's stepmother, Nancy Messinger, when she'd spoken with Renee. She drove to the address she'd been given and parked down the street, gathering her thoughts and figuring out how she was going to approach her.

Renee's father had been the mayor of Red Cedar before Liz and her former husband, Joe, had moved there from San Francisco. She remembered hearing that Don Messinger sold the family ranch many years ago to a developer who had subdivided it and built ranchettes. The transaction made Don Messinger a very wealthy man, wealthy enough that until the time he had died, he had paid his former wife, Renee's mother, a very large monthly alimony payment. Liz had met him once, but had never met Nancy. She decided to use the excuse for visiting Nancy as simply wanting to pay her respects upon learning of the death of her stepdaughter.

She started the van, pulled away from the curb and drove the short distance to Nancy Messinger's home. "Come on, Winston, I'm not particularly looking forward to this given everything I've been told, but I think it's something that needs to be done." Liz and Winston walked up the steps in front of the large house, crossed the porch, and stopped at the front door.

The yard and porch were spotless, recently painted, and beautifully kept up. She rang the doorbell and within moments the door was answered by an imposing woman dressed in black. She wore her grey hair in a blunt cut and no make-up adorned her face. The look she wore on her face was just as severe as the black dress. Hard eyes looked out from a face which was deeply lined. "Yes, may I help you?" the cold and severe looking woman asked.

Without much luck, Liz tried to look into the house to see if it was as austere as the woman in front of her. She could vaguely make out some boxes and things in the hallway, but the woman's edgy tone made her look back at her. It was apparent from the woman's commanding presence and coldness that Liz probably wasn't going to be invited into the house.

"My name is Liz Lucas, and I'm here to express my condolences on the death of your stepdaughter."

"I have no stepdaughter. My husband disinherited both of his daughters. The first one married a Mexican, and the other one moved in with her so she could help take care of her half-breed baby. My husband begged his daughter, Renee, not to marry that man, but she wouldn't listen to him. Broke his heart, it did. I know that's what killed him. She might as well have jammed a knife in her father's heart when she married Bob Salazar. They added insult to injury when Laura took up with them. That was the final nail in Don's coffin. He died not long after. Heard she got murdered, and as far as I'm concerned, good riddance to her. Too bad whoever did it didn't murder Bob and Renee as well. Maybe even their kid. Condolences, lady? I'm not accepting condolences about Laura. Just wish you were giving me condolences for Bob and Renee as well." With that, she slammed the door shut in Liz's face.

Liz looked down at Winston. "Well, I guess we know how she feels about her stepfamily. It's pretty obvious we're not welcome here." They walked back down the steps to her van.

While Liz hadn't found out anything specific as to who had murdered Laura, she couldn't wait to tell Roger what had happened and see what he had to say about it.

On the way home she kept thinking about the experience she'd just had with Nancy Messinger. *That has to be one of the angriest people I've ever met. Think she qualifies as a suspect. Not a far stretch of the imagination to think about her committing murder because she blames her stepdaughters for her husband's death. Wonder what her background is.*

She made a mental note to call Sean and see if he could find out.

CHAPTER TWENTY-ONE

"Hi, I'm Roger Langley. I'm an attorney somewhat new to the area and wanted to introduce myself," Roger said to the attractive redhead seated at the desk in the office of the Lazy K Ranch located in downtown Dillon.

"Nice to meet you. I'm Susie Warren. My brother owns the Lazy K Ranch just outside of town, but I run the day-to-day operations from the office here in Dillon."

"You may be a first for me. I don't think I've ever met a woman who ran a ranch. How did you happen to fall into that?"

She laughed. "Please, have a seat. Would you like a cup of coffee?"

"No, thanks. As I said, I just wanted to stop by and introduce myself. I'm a lawyer and recently opened an office in Red Cedar. My expertise is in criminal defense, but the main firm in San Francisco that I'm associated with has attorneys who are knowledgeable in all areas of law. Here's my business card," Roger said, handing one to her.

"I hope I never need your services, but I'll keep the card. From time to time I do get asked if I know a good attorney," she said smiling. "As far as running a ranch, believe me, it was never on my bucket list, it just kind of happened."

"How does something like that just kind of happen? Seems like there must be more to it than that."

"There always is, isn't there? For me, it was a family member who could no longer run the ranch. Actually, it's no secret. My brother is Mitch Warren. He's the owner of the ranch that's been in the family forever. My father willed the ranch to him because Mitch had overseen it from the time he'd graduated from college. I had no interest in it. My focus was on making it big in the movies. I moved to Los Angeles and other than a walk-on part for a commercial, I never got a call back."

"I'm surprised. I'd think a beautiful woman like you would have a pretty good shot at making it in the movies."

"Thanks for the compliment, but Los Angeles is filled with beautiful women. After being a bar maid for a number of years, I could see the miles begin to show on my face, and my eyes were becoming dead from too many one-night stands and men groping me in the bar. One day I said that's enough and left Los Angeles. I came back here, tail between my legs, so to speak. Everyone in the area knew I'd gone to LA to be a star. It didn't happen. I was simply one of the legions of women who go there and eventually wind up going back home."

"That must have been very difficult for you, but it still doesn't quite tell me how you came to run the ranch."

"I returned here about the time a woman my brother was very much in love with dumped him for someone else. Mitch was a broken man. The ranch started going downhill, and my brother started saying things like 'Everyone would be better off if I was dead' and a lot of other statements that led me to believe he was not only suffering from severe depression, but he was also a suicide risk. He'd been seeing a psychiatrist in San Francisco, because the woman he'd been in love with was a local psychologist, and he couldn't go to her, and because she's well known locally, he didn't want to go to any others in the area. Anyway, I talked to his doctor, and we both agreed Mitch should check himself into a mental treatment facility. Fortunately he was agreeable, and I told him I'd take care of the ranch. Sometimes you just have to rise to the occasion. That's what I did."

"You may have risen to the occasion, but you must have learned a lot about the ranch just by being the daughter and sister of ranchers. Maybe you didn't consciously know it, but I'd bet subconsciously you did."

"That's probably true," Susie said, playing with the coffee cup in her hand. "The funny thing is that I'm good at this, at least that's what the ranch foreman and the CPA for the ranch tell me. Now, I've talked enough about the ranch. I'd like to know why you're really here. I doubt you came all the way over from Red Cedar just to say howdy."

"Not only can you run a ranch, you're very astute. I imagine that's a very good quality to have when you're in charge."

"Let's put it this way. It hasn't hurt, and there are a few ex-employees of the ranch who would probably agree with you, but let's get back to why you're here," she said, setting her coffee cup on her desk and looking steadily at him.

He spread his hands out in the ageless movement of hands that indicate 'You got me.' "All right. You were honest with me, and I'll be the same with you. From what I know your brother was engaged to Renee Messinger. She broke that engagement off to marry a man by the name of Bob Salazar, who is a very good friend of mine."

At the mention of Bob Salazar, Susie's eyes became cold and her lips became a tight grim line. "Bob Salazar. Know the name well. I've never met him, but he's the one responsible for my brother's mental breakdown. That still doesn't explain why you're here."

"I got married the day before yesterday and Bob and his wife, Renee, whom I'm sure you know, attended the wedding and the reception. They have a baby daughter, and Renee's sister, Laura, was taking care of the baby girl at Cindy's Bed & Breakfast in Red Cedar. She was murdered. Cindy heard the baby crying, opened the door of their room, and found Laura. I'm trying to find out everything I can about anyone who might have had a reason to kill Laura."

Susie uncrossed her arms and said, "I'm sorry to hear that. I didn't know about it. I always liked Laura." She sat up straight in her chair. "Wait a minute. Are you inferring that my brother had something to do with it?"

"I'm not inferring anything. I'm simply trying to get a handle on anyone who might have wanted to get back at Bob or Renee and did it through Laura."

She looked at the business card on the desk. "Mr. Langley, I can tell you emphatically that my brother had nothing to do with Laura's death. The foreman of the ranch and I are about the only people who know that each month my brother gets worse. I have twenty-four hour live-in help for him. He's really not capable of making any decisions. I take care of everything having to do with the ranch as well as his care. I think I've told you all you need to know. Please convey my condolences to the Salazar family." She stood up and walked over to the front door and opened it. "It's been nice meeting you. You've found out what you wanted to know. You can go now."

Roger walked over to the door and said, "I've found out what you've told me. I have not found out if your brother managed to get out of the ranch house and take revenge on Renee and Bob Salazar." He walked out the door and involuntarily flinched as it slammed behind him.

CHAPTER TWENTY-TWO

Roger and Liz both got back to the lodge at the same time. She opened the door of her van as he stepped out of his car and hugged her tightly. Winston jumped out of the van and stood next to them, looking up, hoping for an ear scratch. Roger reached down and obliged, while he kissed Liz.

"I hope you're planning something wonderfully comforting for dinner," Roger said. "Spending the evening with Reverend Jacobs is not my idea of a good time."

They walked up the steps to the front door. "You'll be very happy to know I made a cassoulet earlier, and it's been cooking all afternoon. A little French bread and a salad will go with it nicely. I'd offer you a glass of wine, but the reverend might frown on that."

"Right, I don't want to do anything to get on the bad side of a reverend that had to leave Kentucky in the middle of the night because he was caught with an underage girl in the rectory. Liz, somehow I rather doubt he'd even notice."

"That may be true, but everyone else might smell the wine on your breath. Think you better forget about it."

"From what you're saying, I'm getting the distinct impression that even a small glass of wine will be off limits to me tonight," Roger said, grinning at her.

"What? Why are you looking at me like that?" Liz asked.

"I'm just happy we're married, even if it isn't quite the honeymoon I'd planned. Did you find out anything today?"

"Yes. I found out Laura's ex-husband is no longer in Serenity Center. His counselor thought he had an excellent chance to beat his addiction, but that was a week ago, and he hasn't been heard from since. When a patient leaves the Center, they're supposed to check in every forty-eight hours. No one has heard from him since he left the facility. Naturally, they're worried he's relapsed."

"I would be too. I've told you before that a number of the people I've defended over the years had problems with drug addiction. Unfortunately almost fifty percent of the males returned to drug use, even after going through some type of rehabilitation. The women did somewhat better. It wouldn't surprise me to learn Nick has returned to drugs, particularly if Laura didn't want anything more to do with him. Seems like the whole reason he went through the drug program was to reconcile with her. Kind of feel sorry for him. Who knows, he could be in Mexico or anywhere."

"That's what I'm thinking, too. Let me change the subject. Renee's stepmother is one cold fish." She told Roger about her brief meeting with Nancy Messinger.

"I couldn't agree more from what you're telling me. Wonder what Renee's father ever saw in her."

"I have no idea. Maybe it was the fact that she was so devoted to him. I'd really appreciate if you would call Sean and see if he can find out anything about her. Something is bothering me about her and the house, but I just can't put my finger on it."

"Does it qualify as a niggle?" Roger asked, grinning, as they sat down for dinner.

"Yes, but I don't know how. It's just a feeling I have about her. Now, tell me about your afternoon," she said ladling the cassoulet into deep bowls and handing him the warm French bread.

He told her he'd driven over to the Lazy K Ranch office in Dillon and told her about his meeting with Susie. "I can't say we parted good friends. As a matter of fact, I doubt if I could ever again get in that office."

"Was she really quite beautiful?" Liz asked.

"Yes. I'm sure she was the most beautiful young woman around here when she was younger, but she's a little hard around the edges now."

"Sounds like it's pretty much the same thing that happened to my friend Judy. She was sitting in a movie director's office in Los Angeles getting ready to read for a part when she looked around her and realized that every other woman in the office was just as beautiful as she was. She walked out and never looked back. I don't think Judy ever regretted doing it. Yeah, trying to make it in Hollywood is a tough life," Liz said.

"Probably true, but it sounds like Susie has adapted quite well to running the ranch. I didn't see a wedding ring on her finger, so I don't know what the status is on that, but she's quite bright. Even if Mitch isn't in any shape to run the ranch right now, it's in good hands."

"What do you think, Roger? Could Mitch have done it?"

"Susie would certainly like for me to think he was physically and mentally unable to do it. I don't know. Maybe she's covering for him. That's not unusual. I never saw him, so I really don't know if he's as bad off as she says. For the sake of argument, one could assume that he read in the paper about the wedding and reception and that the Salazar family was going to stay at Cindy's Bed & Breakfast. He could have driven over and killed Laura. She'd open the door for him. Of course she'd probably open the door for her ex-husband as well."

"So we're still going round and round in circles."

"Fraid so. And who knows, if it was the Reverend Jacobs, she might open the door for a man of the cloth. Liz, that cassoulet was fabulous. Slow-cooked pork, chicken, beans. My tummy is very happy at the moment, and it better be since it's almost time for me to go to the Bible Study class conducted by the reverend."

"How do you know it's not closed to outsiders?"

"Sean told me there was a big notice that it was open to the general public and they were more than welcome. He said he thought it was kind of a ploy to pull in new members. While I'm thinking of Sean, let me call him and ask him to do some research on Renee's stepmother, and then I have to leave. It'll take me about a half an hour to get to Dillon, and I don't want to be late to the Bible Study class."

CHAPTER TWENTY-THREE

Roger drove to Dillon and easily found the reverend's church. There was a large sign in front of it that read "God's Holy Covenant Church." In the yard in front of the mega church was a fifty foot tall flagpole with the American flag slowly waving in the breeze. The rectory and the picket fence in front of it appeared to have recently received a fresh coat of white paint. Bright red roses trailed along the fence. Baskets hung from the wraparound porch with pink and purple geraniums spilling over them. It was apparent that Reverend Jacobs' home was well taken care of, probably by devoted parishioners. A shiny new SUV was in the driveway of the rectory. It looked like business at the church was booming.

He parked his car in the church parking lot and followed several people into a room in a wing of the church which looked like it housed meeting rooms. There was a sign next to a door that said "Bible Study – All Are Welcome."

Roger walked in and sat down, nodding to several people who then walked over to him and warmly welcomed him. He looked around and saw that there were easily over a hundred people seated in the room waiting for the reverend and the weekly Bible Study class to begin. In a few minutes there was a commotion at the entrance to the room, and a man Roger assumed was the reverend walked in with two other men. From their deferential manner, they appeared to be aides. The reverend walked to the podium and began to speak, putting his coffee cup on a shelf inside the podium.

"First of all, let me introduce myself," the man said in a deep rich southern voice. "I am the Reverend Lou Jacobs of God's Holy Covenant Church. For those of you who are returning to our group, it's wonderful to see you continue with our study of the Bible. For those of you who are new to the church, welcome. Each week we pick a different topic from the Bible and explore it. All are welcome to speak. I strongly advise that you read the Bible at home and spend some quiet time praying over what you've read. This really helps us in our study of the Bible. For several weeks now we've been exploring the Ten Commandments.

"The Bible described the Ten Commandments as being given to the Israelites by God at Mount Sinai. Reference to the Ten Commandments appears twice in the Hebrew Bible, first at Exodus 10:1-17 and then at Deuteronomy 5:4-21. Tonight we will explore the Commandment, Thou Shalt Not Kill."

Well, that's fitting, Roger thought, *considering why I'm here. This should be interesting.*

The next three hours were spent dissecting the commandment and all of its ramifications such as does the prohibition against killing extend to animals, plants, and so on. The reverend was very clear that it certainly meant not taking the life of another human being. At the end of the three hours the reverend ended the study session with a prayer and then stepped away from the podium. He was instantly surrounded by parishioners and others who had questions. It was obvious his parishioners loved him as they hung on every word he said.

Roger had been drinking coffee during the study session and noticed others washing their coffee cups and putting them back in a cabinet. On his way to the sink in the corner he walked by the podium and remembered that he'd seen the reverend drinking from it several times during the evening. He picked it up and took it over to the sink, intending to wash it along with his cup. Roger looked in the bottom and noticed there was some clear liquid in it that didn't look anything like coffee. He glanced around and saw that no one was looking at him, so he quickly stuck his finger into the liquid and tasted it. He had to stop himself from choking and disrupting the group. There was no doubt in Roger's mind that Reverend Jacobs had been drinking straight vodka.

I don't know how much credence I can put in anything the reverend said tonight about not killing when he's been secretly drinking straight vodka from a coffee cup while standing in front of a hundred or so parishioners. He sure isn't quite the pure man of God he'd like everyone to think he is.

People were filing out of the room and Roger happened to be one of the last to leave. The reverend and his two aides were walking just ahead of Roger and he clearly overheard the reverend take the Lord's name in vain when he referred to one of the people who had attended tonight's meeting.

Well, if he broke the commandment about taking the Lord's name in vain, who's not to say he broke the commandment about killing someone. Don't think I'd believe anything he said, not from what I've seen tonight.

CHAPTER TWENTY-FOUR

That evening Liz emailed Jonah and Brittany, thanking them for attending the wedding and for all their help. She never knew what time it was in Dubai, where Jonah was based, so she asked him to email her when he had a minute to let her know he'd returned safely. Brittany had already sent Liz an email that she'd gotten back to Palm Springs safe and sound. Just as she stood up from her computer desk her cell phone rang. She looked at the monitor and saw it was Sean.

"Hi, Sean. How did you know to call me on my phone and not Roger's?"

"When he called me a few hours ago he said he was going to the reverend's Bible Study class, and that if I found out anything, I should call you on your cell phone."

"Does that mean you found out something about Nancy Messinger?"

"Well, yes and no. I found out she worked for Don Messinger as his secretary for about a year before he divorced his wife and married her. I guess he and his former wife weren't getting along, and Nancy was there for him. Happens all the time. I can only assume he married her because she worshipped him. I talked to several people who had known her husband, and that was the general consensus. She waited on him hand and foot and did everything she could for him. Guess he got to liking it, and it seems his wife wasn't doing that for him."

"I've not met Renee's mother, but I have a sense she's not like that. Renee certainly isn't. What else did you find out?"

"Not much. When they met it was before Facebook or Twitter or any of the social media sites, and it's much more difficult to find out things about people prior to the advent of social media. Bottom line is she comes from a small nearby town. Her parents are deceased, and she was an only child. She wasn't married prior to her marriage to Don Messinger, and she has no children. Other than that, I didn't find out much."

"Did you check out Don Messinger?"

"Yes. He owned a ranch, sold it for a great deal of money to a developer, and then he began playing the stock market and investing in this and that. He had a small office in Red Cedar, and that's where Nancy worked. She continued to work in the office a couple of hours a day until he died."

"Did you find out the cause of his death?"

"Yes. Evidently he had a history of heart problems and died from a massive heart attack. He was estranged from Renee and Laura, so there wasn't a funeral service or a celebration of life ceremony, even though he'd been the Mayor of Red Cedar many years ago. Nancy had him cremated, and that's about it. Since I found nothing about her purchasing a place for him in a cemetery or a memorial park, I imagine she probably still has his ashes in the house, or maybe she's got some kind of a shrine in the back yard. People do some strange things. You never know what to expect."

"Thanks, Sean. Naturally I wish more could have been turned up on her, but given my brief meeting with her, I'm not surprised. I'm sure you would have told me if you'd found out any character flaws that she was treated for, like an addiction or mental illness."

"Of course. That's part of the overall search. No, she's clean as a whistle. The only thing I kept hearing was what a cold person she was, and how she totally worshipped Don, almost to the point of obsession."

"Have to wonder if she adored him enough to kill a stepdaughter."

"Could be Liz, could be. Stranger things have happened. I just keep getting a vision of this cold ugly woman – I did see her photograph – in her home with her husband's ashes. Kind of gave me the creeps."

"Me too. One more thing. Do you have any idea how much she inherited from her husband when he died?"

"Yes. She filed a Will, and it's a matter of public record. She inherited twelve million dollars from him."

"Wow! I wonder what she's doing with it. There's nothing about her or the house to indicate she has that kind of money. That's weird. Again, Sean, thanks."

"No problem. I'll look into his finances in the morning. Let me know if you need anything else."

*****

"That's the last time I'm going to a Bible Study class at that man's church," Roger said, as he walked in the door.

"I gather it wasn't your finest hour," Liz said.

"My finest hour? Try my three non-finest hours topped off by the fact that you wouldn't let me have a glass of wine with dinner tonight, and the good reverend was secretly drinking straight vodka from a coffee cup."

"You're kidding! Sit down and tell me everything," she said.

He related his experiences of the evening to her and concluded by saying that although he didn't have anything to base it on other than he thought the reverend was a sham, he still considered him a suspect. She told him what Sean had said when he called her. They each looked at the other one with a "where do we go from here look" on their respective faces.

"Well, it looks like both of our nights were rather unproductive. I found out a couple of things about the reverend, but nothing that ties him to Laura's death, and you found out just what you'd suspected, that Nancy Messinger is a cold fish of a woman who idolized her husband. Wonder how much she inherited? Did Sean mention that?"

"Yes. She received twelve million dollars. For the life of me, I can't figure out what she's done with it. Sean said he'd look into it and call me tomorrow."

"If anyone can find out, Sean's the one. I'm whipped. I had a call when I was on the way home and one of my clients needs to see me tomorrow. Evidently it's an emergency. I have a meeting with him at 1:00 tomorrow afternoon. Sorry, we seem to be getting farther and farther away from our honeymoon. I promise I'll make it up to you."

"I promise I'll let you," Liz said with a smile on her face.

CHAPTER TWENTY-FIVE

The next morning Liz remembered she'd promised Renee she'd go over to her house that afternoon and help her sort through some papers of Laura's. She'd told Liz it was just too hard on her mother to do it, and she thought Liz might get a better sense of who Laura was if she went through them with her. Liz sensed she simply wanted someone with her when she did it. She suspected it was just as hard for Renee as it would be for her mother.

She looked at her watch and decided she better figure out what she was going to have for dinner since she was afraid she might get tied up with Renee and make it back just in time for dinner. She remembered she had some chicken thighs in the refrigerator and started taking out the ingredients she'd need to make coq au vin. She knew it was one of Roger's favorites and it had been a long time since she'd made it. While she was getting the ingredients together for the slow cooked dinner, her cell phone rang. She looked at the caller I.D. and saw it was Gertie.

"Good morning, Gertie. How are you?"

"Hon, if I was any better I'd be twins. Had a coupla new eaters here yesterday and thought ya' might be interested in what they had to say."

"You know I'm always interested in anything you have to tell me.

I'm all ears."

"Well, there were two guys in here fer' dinner last night. Never seen 'em before, so I introduced myself. Matter of fact one of 'em was purty cute, but that's another story. Anyway, I asked 'em what they were doin' in town, and they said they'd been doin' a little work over at the Messinger home. Yer' ears wiggle when ya' heard that, Liz?"

"They sure did, Gertie. Did you find out what kind of work they were doing?"

"Well, yes and no. They told me they were doin' some gold leafin' at the house, but they said that's all they could tell me 'bout it cuz they'd been sworn to secrecy by Mrs. Messinger. Make any sense to you, Liz?"

"Absolutely none. The only thing I know about gold leaf is that it's often used on picture frames. I think some jewelry has gold leaf applied to it but two men working in a house and can't say what they're doing? That's really strange. Did they tell you anything else?"

"No, nuthin' other than they'd been there for a day and a half and had jes' finished the job. They was kind of celebratin'. Said somethin' 'bout it bein' pure 23 karat gold leaf, and their boss was real happy cuz it was a really pricey job. Matter of fact I was curious, so I looked it up on the Internet last night. Lawdy, that stuff is going fer 'round $1,000 bucks an ounce. I'm as curious as a cat."

"If it's any consolation, I am too. I can't think of any reason why two workmen would be in a house for a day and a half doing some job with pure gold leaf. I don't think anyone has that many picture frames."

"Well, I'll leave the info in yer' hands. If ya' figger it out, give me a call. Jes' thought ya' might be interested."

"You know I am, Gertie, but this really has me puzzled. I guess maybe a jeweler could give me information about the various uses of gold leaf. Other than that I don't know where else I can go to find out information about it."

"Why don't ya' give Rich Yates a call? He owns the Yates Jewelry Shop in town. Don't think Roger bought that knuckle buster yer' wearing from our local jeweler, but if ya' give him a call, tell him Gertie referred ya."

"I'll call him right now. Again, Gertie, thanks."

*****

"Yates Jewelry Shop" the male voice on the other end of the line said.

"Hello. My name is Liz Lucas, er Liz Langley. Sorry, I was recently married, and I'm not used to my new name. Anyway, I'm the owner of the Red Cedar Spa and Lodge. Gertie over at the diner suggested I call you. I have a strange request. Do you know of any reason why someone would need two men to work in a residential home with gold leaf for a day and a half?"

"I'm sorry, Ms. Langley, but is this some kind of prank call? I've never heard of anyone needing that much gold leaf."

"No. This is very legitimate." She didn't mention any names but gave Rich Yates the basics of why she was calling him.

"Quite frankly, I can't think of any reason why someone would need that much gold leaf. It's commonly used on small pieces of jewelry and in some art works. There are large figures of Buddha that are known to be covered in gold-leaf, but I haven't heard of any that are recent. I would think if something was being gold-leafed and required a day and a half worth of work from two men it would be newsworthy. Something else to think about is why workmen would be using it. I could understand it more if it was a jeweler or artisan, but workmen? It makes no sense to me at all. I will tell you one thing though. If workmen were applying gold leaf in quantities that required two of them to do it for a day and a half, you're talking about a great deal of money that would be needed to buy that much gold leaf, truly a lot of money. I know I'm not being much help, but that's about the best I can do."

"Thank you very much. I have no idea what this is about, but the fact it could involve a great deal of money is a start. Again, thanks for your time, and the next time I need a jeweler I'll be in to see you."

"I'll look forward to it, and if you do find out what someone is doing with that much gold leaf, I'd love to know about it."

"Consider it done," she said, ending the call, more baffled than ever by the gold leaf mystery.

CHAPTER TWENTY-SIX

Roger had gone downstairs to do some work in his new home office in the remodel he and Liz had done to the lodge before they were married. Two existing storerooms had been converted into an office and a "man cave" for Roger along with floor to ceiling windows being installed, allowing him to enjoy the ocean view.

While Roger was working Liz decided to prep the coq au vin and then put it in the slow cooker to finish cooking. She decided if she got tied up when she went to Renee's, it wouldn't matter. The longer the chicken dish cooked, the more the flavors blended. *Chicken, mushrooms, wine. Mmmm! Who wouldn't like that?* she thought.

Once again she praised the original owner of the lodge for having the foresight to install a walk-in pantry. She was just beginning to get the ingredients out of it for the coq au vin when her cell phone rang again.

"Good morning, Sean. You're always the bearer of information of some type I can use. Find out anything about Nancy Messinger's finances?"

"Yes, Liz, but I don't know what you're going to do with this information. It's some of the strangest I've ever run across."

"You're making me very curious."

"Here it is. I was able to get all of Nancy Messinger's bank deposits and disbursements for the last year. Before her husband died, there were the usual expenditures for food, clothes, utilities, you know, the normal household things. As far as deposits, I've already told you he was a wealthy man. He had monthly dividends from different investments that were quite substantial. When he died, his wife inherited the investments and liquidated them, resulting in about twelve million dollars being added to her account. For several months after his death, her expenditures didn't change."

"Why do I get the feeling the other shoe is about to drop, Sean?"

"Because it is. In the last few weeks, there have been some very strange expenditures. One was paid to a company called A-One Gold Leaf in the amount of one million dollars. I don't know much about gold leaf other than it goes for around a thousand dollars an ounce, so that's a lot of ounces."

"That's about the strangest thing I've ever heard. Why would she buy that much gold leaf?"

"Good question. I asked myself the same thing. I called the company and talked to the owner. I used the excuse that I was her CPA, and I needed to know the purpose of the purchase for my records. I've got to give the guy credit. He was completely discreet and wouldn't tell me a thing. Usually I can unearth something, but not in this case."

"Did you find out anything else?"

"Yes. She bought an urn that had emeralds and rubies embedded in it. I talked to the jeweler who had set the stones in the urn. It was made of 24 karat gold, and you can just imagine how expensive that alone was, plus the cost of the gems."

"Commissioning an urn that close to Don's death indicates to me she was going to use it for his ashes. From the way everyone said she was almost obsessed with him, I'm not completely surprised by that. Did you find out the name of the mortuary that cremated the body?

I'd like to know if she said anything to them about an urn."

"I'm one step ahead of you there, Liz. I called the Eternal Life Memorial Home. They're the ones who handled Don's cremation. I told them the same thing I'd told the gold leaf guy about needing to know the details, so I could keep the accounting records straight. Had better luck with them than I did the gold leaf guy."

"What did you find out?"

"Don Messinger was cremated and Nancy picked his ashes up from the memorial home the day they became available. The director of the home was the one who took care of her, and he told me something he thought was quite strange, and I agree."

"I'm beginning to not be surprised by anything strange this woman does. What did he have to say?"

"He said she held the urn in her hands when he gave it to her and said to it, 'Darling, you won't be in this one for very long. I'm having one made for you of gold, rubies, and emeralds. You deserve it.' Guess that was the urn she had made."

"I'm afraid to even hear the answer to this, but is there anything else?"

"Yes. She bought an antique Savonarola chair from an auction house in New York. Do you know what that is?

"I've heard of it, but I can't place it."

Sean said laughing, "Glad you've heard of it, because I didn't have a clue what it was. It's a wooden chair that's designed in the form of an X. In times past it was used in military campaigns because it could be folded. The one she bought was from the 18th century, but here's the kicker. The auction house told me that the Savonarola chairs are so uncomfortable that most people who buy them today use a padded cushion when they sit on them. Nancy Messinger had a special cushion made for it out of silk."

"Well, that's understandable. If it was nothing but wood, having a padded cushion for it seems like the first reasonable thing you've told me she's bought recently."

"I don't think having a padded cushion with diamonds is all that reasonable," Sean said wryly.

"What?" Liz practically screamed through the phone. "Are you telling me there were diamonds in the cushion?"

"No, not in the cushion. I talked with the pillow cushion seamstress who had been instructed to enclose each of the diamonds in white gauze and attach them to the fringe on the sides of the pillow. The seamstress was pretty excited about it. She told me the diamonds were brought to her by an armed guard, and the guard was in the room with her the whole time while she sewed the diamonds onto the fringe of the pillow. He paid her and took the pillow with him when he left. She didn't know why someone would do that, but she was happy to help. I haven't been able to get ahold of the jeweler who sold her the diamonds."

"Sean, I know you've seen a lot of things during your time as the chief investigator for Roger's law firm, but I have to ask you this. Have you ever been involved in a case quite like this?"

"No. I don't know what to make of it. I'm just telling you what I found out. Guess it's up to you to figure out the relevance of it."

"Thanks. You have a lot more confidence in my abilities than I do."

"My other line is ringing, Mrs. Langley. Talk to you soon."

*****

She ended the call and realized a voice mail had come in on the lodge line. She'd been so intent on what Sean was telling her she'd missed it. She pressed the replay button and listened to it.

"Liz, it's Mike Hadley at Serenity Center. I have some news about Nick Hutchinson. He's in jail in San Francisco. Evidently he was arrested in a drug bust. It bothered me we hadn't heard from him. I have friends in a few of the police forces ariybd the state, and I emailed them to see if they knew anything about him. When I got the email he'd been arrested and was in jail I emailed my friend back and asked him when Nick had been arrested. I got one of those replies that someone is out of the office until a certain date. I don't have his cell phone or a private email address. I seem to remember your husband works for a law firm that's based in San Francisco. He might be able to find something out. Sorry I missed you. Call me if I can help, but that's all I know."

She hung up the phone, trying to digest what Sean and Mike had told her. The first thing that needed to be done was to find out when Nick had been arrested. She walked downstairs to Roger's home office.

"Hello, my beautiful wife. I heard you talking on the phone. Anything you want to share with me?"

"I want to share everything with you," she said sitting down on the grey and rust plaid upholstered chair next to his desk. "I had a long talk with Sean, and then I had a message from Mike over at the Serenity Center." She told him about both of the calls.

"Liz, I'll handle finding out about Nick. Remember Jim, my friend with the San Francisco Police Department. He was the one who helped you with that tarot card murder. As I remember, he even said he was indebted to you for helping them crack a credit card scamming ring they'd been working on. I'll give him a call. Do you want me to do anything about what Sean told you?"

"No. Renee asked me to come over to her house this afternoon and help her go through some of Laura's papers. She thought it would be too traumatic for her mother. I think the real reason she wants me there is that it's too traumatic for her. Anyway, let me pick her brain and see if any of this latest information about Nancy rings a bell, although since Renee's been estranged from both her father and

Nancy for quite a while, it probably won't, but maybe I'll get some ideas."

"I have that meeting this afternoon with a client. Want me to fix something for dinner when I get home?"

"No. I thought we'd have coq au vin. I've prepped it, and I'll put everything in the crock pot and just let the flavors blend all afternoon. I can make a salad and cook some noodles to go with it. Should be perfect when we're ready to eat. Good luck with your client, sweetheart. See you later."

"Liz, remember to take your two friends with you, your gun and Winston."

"I love you, but you're beginning to sound like a broken record. I will. Promise," she said, walking out the door.

CHAPTER TWENTY-SEVEN

Liz pressed the doorbell on the large ranch style house that Bob and Renee had recently purchased on the outskirts of Dillon. They'd previously been living in an older Arts and Crafts style home, but when Renee found out she was pregnant, she convinced Bob that their daughter-to-be would need a large yard for her toys and pets. Liz laughed to herself as she looked around the yard. Celia was only a few months old, and already one side of the yard had a swing set along with riding toys that were scattered here and there.

She smiled and thought, *not the first time a child's been spoiled when it's the first child for a parent who just turned fifty. I'd be willing to bet that little girl will get whatever she wants, and she'll have Bob wrapped around her finger in no time. Hope Renee is strong enough to counterbalance Bob's tendencies.*

The front door was opened a moment later by a woman about Liz's age. "Come in, come in, you must be Liz. I'm Camille Messinger, Laura's mother. Congratulations on your recent marriage. I'm sorry you have to deal with all of this this during a time when you should have been enjoying your honeymoon."

"It's nice to meet you. I'd like to express my condolences. I am so sorry. What a senseless thing to have happen. I never met Laura, but I'm a mother, and I can only imagine what you must be going through," she saud as she walked into the house and was greeted by Renee.

"I'm so glad you could come. I haven't gone through anything yet. It's so painful, and yet I know it needs to be done. I'm hoping there will be something in Laura's papers and things that can help identify who murdered her. I keep thinking if it's Nick, maybe there's an angry letter in there from him. Have you found out anything?"

"Yes, actually I've found out quite a bit, but I'd rather get this over with first. We can talk later. How do you want to go about it?"

Renee and her mother exchanged a look. "Liz," Camille said, "I don't think either one of us can do this without getting so emotional we probably wouldn't be of much use. Renee told me you'd asked her if there was anything you could do for her. Would you go through Laura's papers? You'll know if something's important. I think if either of us did it, we'd dissolve in tears."

"Of course. I understand, and I'd be happy to do it for you. Where are her things? And do you want me to go through her clothes as well?"

Renee began to walk down the hall, indicating Liz was to follow her. "I put a pile of papers and correspondence on her desk. Why don't you start there? When you finish with that, call me. Laura had a habit of sticking letters and things in her pockets to be read later. I'm wondering if she stuck something important in one of them and forgot about it. I know it's a lot to ask, but I'd be forever grateful if you could check her clothes, too."

"Certainly. Why don't you and your mother take care of Celia or do whatever you need to do. I'll let you know when I've finished with the correspondence."

"Thanks. We'll just be down the hall," Renee said as she walked out of the room.

For the next hour and a half, Liz opened and read everything that was in the pile of correspondence that Renee had put on the desk for her. There was nothing unusual in the stack of papers. Magazine renewals, some past due bills from when Laura and Nick had been married, things that Laura had printed up from the Internet to be read later such as articles on nursing programs and the care of infants. Her death remained as much of a mystery to Liz as it had been when she'd first begun searching for the murderer. When she finished, she stood up and walked to the door of the bedroom.

"Renee. I'm finished with the correspondence. What would you like me to do now?"

Renee came down the hall and walked into the room. "If you don't mind, I'd really appreciate it if you could go through her clothes and the things in the closet. It's not very large, and she wasn't a big clothes person, so there really aren't many clothes in it. She wore a nurse's uniform most of the time until the county hospital had to lay off a number of personnel due to budget cuts. I'd suggest you concentrate on the pockets. Tomorrow I'm having someone come and take her clothes to a battered woman's shelter. Maybe they'll help someone. I hope so. I'd like to think if she had to die, at least her life meant something," Renee said as tears began to trickle down her face.

"Since she was a nurse, I'm sure she helped a lot of people. You probably just didn't know about them. I'll get started and call you if I need you."

Liz decided if she was going to do this, she was going to be thorough, so she carefully took each piece of clothing out of the closet, checked the pockets, and hung it back up on a hangar in the closet. When she was about halfway through, she pulled a heavy winter coat out of the closet and noticed what looked like a photo album in the back of the closet. She took it out and opened it. It was clearly a family album with photographs of Renee and Laura, Camille, and a number of photos of Don Messinger from the time he was a young boy to the last one which was a photo of Renee, Laura and Don. From the looks of Renee, it didn't seem more than a few years old.

I wonder if Renee knows about it. She's never mentioned it. Funny Laura would have stashed it in the back of her closet.

Liz went through the pockets of the coat and ran her hands over the inside lining. She heard something crackle and ran her hand over the inside again, finding an interior pocket. She pulled out a large unopened letter addressed to Laura Hutchinson. In the upper left hand corner was Don Messinger's return address. Liz's heart began to race. She took a deep breath and carefully opened the letter. She read it and reread it. She put it down and stood for a moment, composing herself before asking Renee to come into the room.

"Renee, I found something I think you should see. Can you come in here?"

"What is it?" Renee asked as she quickly entered the room.

"I think you better sit down. I want to read you a letter your father sent to Laura, which I found in an interior pocket of this winter coat. It was unopened and like you said, she probably stuck it in her pocket so she could read it later, and then she forgot about it."

Renee sat down on the bed and looked at Liz expectantly as she began to read the letter.

"My darling Laura, I don't think I have much time left as I sense my life is coming to an end. I've made some very bad mistakes in my life, and I hope you and your sister can forgive me for what I've done to the two of you. I was wrong about Bob Salazar. He's a good man, and I was very, very stupid to let him come between Renee and me, and yes, between you and me as well. I love you both so much. Please tell Renee how sorry I am and how much I regret hurting her and hurting you.

"I very much want to reconcile with both of you and try and make up for the pain I've caused you. Even though I said I didn't want to see my granddaughter when she's born, that's not true. I definitely want to see her if Renee will allow me to. Turning to something else. I fear that Nancy is becoming insane. I'm sure you're asking yourself why I think that about her. It's not just one thing, but a lot of things. She's still as devoted to me as ever, but I find her talking to herself and saying things that make no sense at all to me or anyone else for that matter. I'm sure you and Renee often wondered why I married her. It was because of her devotion to me, but in the last few years I've found it stifling and more like an obsession with her. She demands to know where I am every minute of the day. Sometimes I feel like I can't breathe.

"I'm writing this to you rather than Renee, because I was afraid she'd throw it away, unopened, if she saw it was from me. When you've had a chance to read this and talk to your sister, please call me at the cell phone number I've written below. I bought a special one that Nancy doesn't know about. Please, please, please forgive me for what I've done.

"Also Laura, included with this letter is an original Last Will and Testament signed by me and two witnesses, gardeners of mine. It's probably rather ironic that they're Mexican given my past actions towards my son-in-law. Anyway, if for some reason you and Renee decide you don't want anything to do with me, at least make sure that at the time of my death, this Will is filed with the probate court. I have provided for Nancy by leaving her one million dollars. I am leaving you and Renee the rest of my estate, which is probably in the area of eleven million dollars. Pure and simple, I love you both. Again, please forgive me. Your Loving Father, Don Messinger."

Renee stared at Liz, sobbing, and trying to speak. "What is the date of the letter?"

"It's dated March 23rd of this year. That's the same date that's on the Will. Laura probably would have been wearing a coat like this at that time of year, so it's not surprising she would have stuck the letter in there. I imagine she simply forgot about it. When did your father die?"

"He died April 3rd. We killed him. We didn't know it, but we killed him by not calling him. Oh no, I can't bear any more. First Laura, and now this. We killed him as surely as someone killed Laura. Maybe that's why she was killed. Maybe it was just a random thing, a kind of a karmic justice."

Liz walked over to Renee and put her arms around her. "You didn't know anything about this. What's wonderful is that your father did want to reconcile with both you."

"But he'll never know how much I wanted that," Renee said as tears continued to flow down her cheeks. Liz reached out and held her for a long time while she cried bitter tears of despair.

CHAPTER TWENTY-EIGHT

It took Renee the better part of an hour to finally stop crying and achieve some semblance of normalcy. Her face was a combination of red splotches from crying and white from shock. Liz and Renee each became very quiet, lost in thought about the implications of the letter and the Will. They heard Camille cooing in the other room as she took care of Celia. Winston had been quietly sitting in the room while Liz looked through the papers and then the closet. Several times he'd walked over to Renee and put his head on her knee while she mindlessly petted him, tears continuing to run down her cheeks.

Liz was a firm believer in dog therapy and privately thought that Winston might have been the reason that Renee was finally able to get herself under control. She knew Winston was astute enough to realize that Renee was in a great deal of emotional pain.

It's pretty hard to stay wrapped in your troubles when a dog is begging for attention. She smiled at Winston thinking he had to be the most perceptive dog she'd ever been around.

"I need to tell my mother about this," Renee said. "I think it will make her happy to know Dad wanted to reconcile with Laura and me. Do you mind if I call her in here?" Renee asked.

"Wait just a moment. There are some other things I need to tell you." She filled Renee in on her conversations with Sean and Gertie as well as the message Mike Hadley had left on the lodge answerphone. "You can see from what I just told you that there are a lot of things we need to consider, and I haven't even had time to think about the consequences of your father's Will. I think that will be a subject for Roger and Bob to handle. I'm sure this isn't the first time a new Will has surfaced after the estate has been settled, and I'm also sure there's some legal precedent for it."

"Do you have any idea what Nancy will do if that money is taken away from her? And what about the money she's already spent?" Renee asked, color beginning to come back into her face.

"I rather doubt she's going to be doing cartwheels for joy when she's told. I just had a thought. Have you stayed in touch with any of your father's neighbors? Is there someone you could call to find out what's been going on at the house lately?"

"Yes. I still talk to Sally and Jeff Gruber regularly. They've lived in the house next door ever since Dad and Nancy bought it. As a matter of fact, they were even at our wedding. They're very nice. Why?"

"Good. In that case it wouldn't be particularly unusual for you to call them. You might even use the ploy that you didn't know if they'd heard about Laura. I know that's probably going to be painful for you, but I'd like to know if the Grubers have noticed anything unusual going on at Nancy's house. I still can't figure out why she bought all that gold leaf."

"If you feel it's important, I'll call them right now. By the way, they never liked Nancy. They thought she was really weird, and something else that kind of goes along with what Dad said in his letter is that the last time I talked to them they mentioned they thought Nancy was getting stranger and stranger, if that was possible."

When Liz took her cell phone out of her purse and handed it to Renee, she saw the gun Roger had insisted she carry. *Well, with the gun in my purse and Winston in the room, I'm doing exactly what Roger wanted me to do. Being careful.*

"Hi, Sally, it's Renee Salazar. I'm calling on a sad note. I don't know if you've heard that my sister Laura was murdered. The police have no idea who did it, but they're investigating several suspects." She listened for a moment. "Thanks, I appreciate that. I thought you might have been told, but I was calling just in case you hadn't heard. I'm wondering if Laura's death had any effect on Nancy. Anything going on over there?"

She listened for several moments and then said, "Thanks for telling me. I have no idea why the A-One Gold Leaf truck would have been there for a day and a half. And you said several delivery trucks have also been there lately along with an armed guard. That's kind of unusual, isn't it?" Again she listened to Sally and then said, "I really don't know what's going on with her. As you know, we're estranged, so I know nothing about her activities. Well, I hear Celia and better go take care of her. Give my best to Jeff. Talk to you later."

Renee ended the call and turned to Liz. "You probably got a good sense of what she was saying by my responses, but there were two things she said you might not have heard, and I think they're odd. The first is that several times recently late at night she and Jeff would have sworn they heard hymns and spiritual music coming from her house. The second thing she said was that a truck from Zeke's Candles in San Francisco was there a couple of days ago and she saw two men carry all sizes of white pillar candles into the house. She said it took them a couple of hours. She thought it was kind of weird, and I have to agree with her. What do you think?"

Candles, spiritual music, gold leaf. What do they all have in common? I can't for the life of me figure it out, but one thing has become very clear to me. I need to get in that house.

"Renee, I get something called a niggle, for lack of a better word, from time to time. I've really become aware of it when I've tried to figure out who's committed a crime or a murder. I've got a real niggle that's telling me I've got to get into that house. An idea just occurred to me. Let me run it by you and see what you think."

An hour later Renee and Liz agreed that the plan they were going to carry out tomorrow would stand a much better chance of working if their husbands didn't know anything about it. Renee told Liz she'd pick her up at ten the next morning.

"Liz, I feel like I have to tell Mom and Bob about what was in the Will and the letter. I won't mention to them what we're planning to do, but I can't keep that news from them, plus I think it will be a huge relief to both of them. Is that all right with you?"

"Yes. I wouldn't be able to keep something like that from Roger either, so I completely understand. I'd like you to bring me a plastic shopping bag, and I'll put the photo album in it. I'd rather your mother didn't see it, plus I want to remove the photos of everyone except your father from it. I'll give them back to you when we're finished tomorrow."

"I understand completely. I hope this works. This is becoming so bizarre. If Roger hears from his friend in the San Francisco Police Department about Nick, I'd like to know. Depending on the date when Nick was arrested, it will either make him a very viable suspect or take him out of the running. Although I always felt Nick wasn't good enough for Laura, I know she loved him, and I think he loved her to the best of his ability. Unfortunately it looks like the best of his ability wasn't enough to get him off drugs. It's so sad. I'll get the plastic bag and be back in a minute."

When she opened the door she heard Renee say, "Everything okay, Mom?" and Camille answer, "Yes, I just put Celia down and was going to the kitchen to think about what we'd have for dinner."

Renee returned a moment later. "Here you are. I'll see you in the morning. I'll tell Mom you thought I needed to get out for a little while and were taking me to Gertie's Diner, so I'll drive over and pick you up. See you at ten and Liz, thanks again for all your help."

CHAPTER TWENTY-NINE

The next morning when Renee's car rolled to a stop in the lodge's parking lot, Liz said, "Bye, Roger. Renee's here. I'll be back in a little while. Since we're just going to Gertie's Diner, I think I'll leave Winston with you."

"Sure, that will be fine. Don't think you can get in much trouble at Gertie's, but then again, I never know about you," he said laughing and waving to Renee.

"What did you tell Roger?" Renee asked after Liz had gotten in her car.

"Last night I told him what I found in the closet. I didn't tell him about your conversation with Sally Gruber. I was afraid he might get concerned that you and I were planning on trying to see what's going on at Nancy's house. I know he wouldn't approve of that, plus he'd want me to take Winston with me, and I don't think Nancy would be too thrilled about seeing him again. Having him with us would probably insure we couldn't get in the house. I told him you wanted to talk to me about what you should do about your mother and Celia. I said you didn't want to talk where she could overhear the conversation, and so we decided to go to Gertie's for breakfast. And you, what did you tell Bob?"

"Pretty much the same. He wants to talk with Roger to see what can be done about Dad's Will. He was so relieved to hear that Dad wanted to reconcile with us and approved of Bob. I think it had bothered him a lot, much more than he let on."

"Renee, you're the psychologist, not me, but I'm a little concerned that Bob seems to be reluctant to tell you things. I know what you're going to say about it being hard for a man who's fifty and has never been married to suddenly tell a spouse things when he's never had to before. I completely understand, but having been married for a long time, I think it's kind of critical for spouses to share things with one another." She laughed and said, "By that I mean important things. If you don't want to tell him how much you paid for some expensive eye cream you bought, I think that falls into a different category."

"As a psychologist I'm always counseling couples to do exactly what you just described. I've made a decision that when this whole thing gets resolved I'm going to suggest to Bob that we make some promises to one another not to hold things back that could be important. I honestly think he does it to shield me from certain things he feels might be unpleasant. I've never felt that he's deliberately doing it to hurt me."

"I couldn't agree more, and I know it's none of my business, but it might have helped if you'd known a little more about his relationship with Candy and the anonymous phone call that caused him to pull out of the election."

"Believe me, I've thought the same thing these last few days. I still think they could be tied to Laura's death, but I don't want to bring up Candy and the anonymous telephone call and have Bob feel any guiltier than he's already feeling right now."

Well, it doesn't have to be some name-calling thing," Liz said. "You could simply say that based on some things that have recently happened you'd feel a lot better if you and he confided a bit more in each other. Bob's a smart man. I'm sure he's wished he never withheld those things from you. Anyway, I'll get off my soapbox. We're almost there. Let's go over our plan one more time." She laid out the plan they had decided on the day before as Renee parked her car in the Messinger driveway.

Liz and Renee walked up the steps to the front door, Renee holding the photo album. Liz rang the doorbell. A few moments later Nancy opened the door and coldly said, "What do you want, Renee? You know you're not welcome here."

"Nancy, I found a photo album that I've never seen before. It was Laura's. I know we've been estranged, but I'd like to reach out to you. You and I were close at one time, and I would hope maybe, for my father's sake, we could have that relationship again. Anyway, this is a photo album with lots of great pictures of my father. I thought you might want to look at it. I remember some of these were taken when I was a child. I'd like to talk you through the album. I believe you've met my friend, Liz Lucas. She and I were on our way to a late breakfast or an early lunch, and I talked her into letting me stop here. May we come in?"

She was clearly torn between not wanting them to enter her house and her desire to see the photographs of the husband she'd idolized. Her desire to see the photos won. "All right, you can come in for a few minutes, but don't get too comfortable. You won't be here for long."

She turned and walked into the house. Renee looked over at Liz and nodded towards a door off the kitchen. "Let's sit on the couch, Nancy. That way I can be next to you when I explain the photographs to you." The couch faced away from the door Renee had nodded towards.

"Mrs. Messinger," Liz said, "I'm so sorry, but I seem to have eaten something that isn't agreeing with me. Would you mind if I used your bathroom?"

"I'd rather you didn't, but I suppose I probably better let you. It's down the hall on the left." Liz walked down the hall as Renee opened the first page of the photo album and slowly explained where the pictures on the page had been taken and when. Liz knew from the number of pages and what they had pre-agreed on that she only had about seven or eight minutes to see what she could find out about what was going on in the house.

*****

"Of course I'll take my mother-in-law's call," Bob said to his secretary. "Good morning, Camille. I hope Celia is behaving herself."

"As always, but that's not why I called. I should have told you this last night, but with everything else, it didn't seem all that important. I've been thinking about it this morning, and the more I think about it the more worried I am, particularly after Don said in his letter that he thought Nancy had some kind of a mental problem."

"Camille, I don't understand why you're calling. We talked about the letter and the Will last night and decided not to do anything until after we found out who murdered Laura."

"Bob, this isn't about the Will. I'm calling to tell you I overheard a conversation between Renee and Liz late yesterday afternoon. No, that's not quite true. I eavesdropped, so I could hear a conversation Renee and Liz were having. What I heard is causing me some concern, and I thought I better call you and tell you about it. It seems they've cooked up some scheme to go to Nancy's house and have Renee show her photographs of Don and explain them while Liz snoops around the house. They were talking about the basement in Nancy's house and trying to figure out a way for Liz to get in it."

"If Nancy really is crazy," Bob said, "they could both be in danger. I'm a half hour away here in Dillon, but I'll call Roger right now and see if he can go over there. It's pretty close for him. Did they say anything else?"

"Something about a neighbor hearing spiritual music coming from the house and candles being delivered. Celia started crying about then, so I couldn't completely make out everything they were saying."

"I'm on my way there. I'll call Roger now and let you know when I find out something." He raced out the door of his law office, and over his shoulder yelled to his secretary, "Cancel any appointments I have today. I'll call you later." He ran to his car and began speeding towards Red Cedar. As soon as he was on the road, he called Roger.

"Hi, Bob," Roger said. "Liz told me about the Will she found yesterday and that we should probably get together and figure out how you should proceed with this. Thought I'd ask a couple of guys at the firm who are experts in probate law what needs to be done. I also want an…"

Bob interrupted Roger in mid-sentence and said in an urgent tone of voice, "Hold on Roger. Listen to me. Liz and Renee have gone to Nancy's house. They've cooked up some plan for Renee to show Nancy photographs of Don while Liz explores the house and particularly the basement. You need to get over there now. I have a very bad feeling about what they're doing. If you need help, the Gruber's live next door. I'll call them right now."

"On my way. I'll call you when I know something." He ended the call and looked down to where Winston was lying on the floor at his feet.

Of all the times for Liz not to take Winston with her. I can't believe she's doing something like this and never said a word to me. He grabbed his gun, yelled to Winston, and ran out the door. *I just hope I get there in time.*

CHAPTER THIRTY

As soon as Liz was out of Nancy's range of vision she walked to the door that Renee had nodded towards when they entered the house. She turned the doorknob, and the door easily swung away from her, revealing steps that led down to what Liz presumed was the basement Renee had told her about yesterday. She could just make out the steps with the light that was coming from several windows at the tops of the basement walls. Liz didn't talk about her niggle very much, but at the moment it was on high alert. Liz slowly descended the narrow stairwell that was enclosed by walls on both sides. She had no idea what awaited her at the bottom of the stairs.

Her foot hit the basement floor, and she gasped as she looked around at the basement in astonishment. Every square inch of the basement walls were covered in gold leaf, and even the floor had been covered in gold leaf. At the back of the room on top of a gold leaf table was the emerald and ruby encrusted urn Sean had told her about. Liz assumed it held Don's ashes. Candles of every height lined the room. About six feet in front of the urn was the Savonarola chair with its silk cushion and diamond woven fringe. Resting on the cushion was a book entitled *How to Conduct a Séance* and subtitled *Calling Your Husband Back from the Dead*. There was a CD player on another gold leaf table with a stack of CDs on it.

Liz walked over to the CD player and looked at the titles: Séances for Calling Your Spouse; Music to Listen to During a Séance; and

Music to Bring Back a Loved One were just a few of the titles. She shivered involuntarily.

She's crazy, Liz thought. *She's got to be crazy. She bought all this stuff so she could hold séances to reach out and talk to her dead husband. I've never seen or heard of anything like this.*

She was so absorbed in what she was looking at she didn't hear the door open at the top of the stairs or the click of the lock on the door. She never heard Nancy descend the stairs until she heard a voice say, "So now you know what I'm doing. I didn't think you came here the day before yesterday to pay your respects. I knew you were up to something, so I read about you on the Internet. I found out you're an amateur sleuth who's gotten lucky a couple of times solving murder cases. I know you know I killed Laura."

"Nancy, where's Renee?" Liz asked, stepping back from the woman who held a large revolver with a metal object attached to the end of the barrel.

"She's upstairs, resting. I bashed her real good with the butt of my pistol and she's out cold. I'll bring her down here later, so she can permanently join her father for a little while. Rather fitting, don't you think?" she asked, laughing maniacally. "Once I kill her I won't put her in the urn. That one's reserved for Don. After she's spent a little time down here telling her father how sorry she is she married that Mexican, I'll kill her like I did her sister and bury her in the back yard garden."

"So you own a gun with a silencer on it. That's what that thing is on the end of the barrel, isn't it?" Liz asked.

"Yes, this old revolver was Don't favorite. He took it to a gun shop and had them install a silencer on it so he could shoot little animals that would get in our garden from time to time. Critters like rabbits, squirrels, skunks, and every once in a while, a coyote. With the silencer on it, there was no sound other than a 'whoosh' and the neighbors never heard a gunshot when he shot one of them. It came in real handy when I decided to kill Laura. She just opened the door when I knocked, and when she saw the gun in my hand she moved as far away as she could from the crib. I pulled the trigger, and there was no sound of a gunshot, only the 'whoosh' sound. That's why no one at Cindy's Bed & Breakfast ever heard anything, but I suppose you already figured out that the gun that killed Laura must have been equipped with a silencer, given how smart you're supposed to be at solving murders."

"Nancy, you won't get away with this. People know that strange things have been going on here. When Renee and I are missed, they'll come here looking for us."

"Don't think so. Both of you are too smart to tell people you were going to come here. I'll bet neither one of your husbands knows a thing about you being here. And surprise of surprises, you're going into the garden right beside Renee. Can't let you go given how much you know, Ms. Hotshot Amateur Sleuth. This is the last murder case you'll ever work on. Too bad no one will ever know you solved it. The silencer will make sure that no one hears the gunshots. Who knows? Maybe the coyotes will discover both of you. Not much is sacred in a garden when there are wild animals around and living on the edge of town, we've been known to get a lot of them.

"After I put you and Renee in the garden, I'll take her car and roll it off a cliff into the ocean. I can walk the two miles back here. Everyone will assume the two of you were in the car when it went into the ocean. The only thing is they won't be able to find your bodies. The authorities will figure they washed out to sea with the tide. They'll never know you and Renee will be in the garden, and no one would ever think to dig up my yard. Why would they?"

Liz was starting to panic and wished she'd brought her purse with her. If she had access to it, she thought maybe she could have tried to grab the gun Roger insisted she keep in her purse. *And what about Winston?* She wished she'd at least brought him and let him stay in the car. As perceptive as he was, he might have sensed something was wrong. The only thing she could think to do was stall for time. She didn't know what good it would do, but she knew she wasn't quite ready to die.

"Nancy, I have to admit I kind of find all of this fascinating. My first husband died, and I never thought to hold a séance for him. How do you do it?"

"I had to do a lot of research on it, and that's why I've just started to hold them in the last few days. I needed a quiet room with a lot of candles. The gold leaf was my touch. Don deserves the best. Traditionally, three or more people are at a séance, but I found some instances where only one person held it. Every night I sit here playing music and talking to Don. I ask him questions, and the answers are always revealed. I know he's here with me, right here in this room. He didn't want to leave me. It was his anger over his daughters that caused his fatal heart attack. He'd never leave me."

"That's a lot of candles to light. Do you light each one of them every night?"

"Yes, I have more in the garage for when I use these up. Candles are a critically important part of a séance."

"Don't you think the neighbors will wonder what you're doing?"

"No. They're all asleep. The best time to contact the spirits is between 11:30 p.m. and 12:30 a.m. Don's always waiting for me. It's so reassuring to be with him again, but we've talked long enough. I know you're hoping someone will rescue you, but there's no one here but me. Oh, Renee's here, but as hard as I hit her, she won't be available for quite awhile."

Liz took a deep breath and knew that time was running out. She just hoped Roger knew how much she loved him and how happy she'd been to be his wife, even though it had been for only a few short days. She didn't want him to go through the death of another wife, but she didn't know what she could do about it. Nancy held all the cards in her hand in the form of the gun with the silencer.

CHAPTER THIRTY-ONE

Roger parked his car around the block from the Messinger home. He wanted to make sure he wasn't seen. He and Winston turned the corner running and saw a couple he assumed were the Grubers standing in the yard next to Nancy Messinger's house.

He ran over to them and said, "I'm Roger Langley. You must be the Grubers. Do you know anything about what's going on next door?"

"I'm Jeff Gruber. Thank heavens you're here. Bob called and said there might be trouble next door, so I looked in the front window. Renee's lying on the floor in the living room, and she's not moving. See those windows at the base of the house? They're basement windows. When I didn't see Nancy in the living room, I looked in one of them. I saw a woman and Nancy standing in the basement, and Nancy had a gun pointed at the woman. Looked like there was gold everywhere. Dangedest thing I've ever seen."

"Is there a door leading to the basement from outside the house?" Roger asked, taking his gun out of its holster.

"No. You'll have to go in the house through the front door. The door leading to the basement is just off the kitchen," Jeff Gruber said. "Want me to come with you?"

"No. I've got pretty good protection here," he said, looking at Winston who was quivering. Anything else I should know?"

"No. I'll call the police."

"When you call, ask for the chief of police and tell him Liz Langley's in trouble. She knows him," he said over his shoulder as he and Winston sprinted towards Nancy's house. He put his hand on the front doorknob, and it easily opened. A moment later he and Winston were in the house. He saw Renee lying on the floor. He could see her chest move and knew she was breathing, but he couldn't take the time to help her. It was critical for him to get downstairs to where Liz was being held at gunpoint.

Roger walked quietly to the door the Grubers had mentioned, Winston beside him. He tried to open the door, but it was locked. He heard the squeak it made from his effort and jumped to one side, pulling Winston with him. A bullet whizzed silently through the door and lodged in the wall across from it. Roger jumped back in front of the door and kicked it as hard as he could. Fortunately, the hinges were old, and it easily flew open.

He heard Liz's voice. "Whoever's there, please help me. I knocked Nancy down when she turned her back on me and shot at the door, and I was able to get her gun. I have it aimed at her. Please, help me," Liz said in a terrified voice.

Roger and Winston raced down the stairs. Winston ran over to Liz and sat in front of her, growling and snarling at Nancy who was laying prone on the golden floor. Roger aimed his pistol at Nancy and said, "Liz, tell me what happened."

"She's the one who killed Laura. She admitted it. She blames Laura for Don's death. She told me when Laura told Don she'd decided to live with Renee and Bob, it was the last straw. She thinks it put Don over the edge, because he had his fatal heart not long after."

"Liz, the Grubers called Seth. He should be here any minute.

What's with this room? I've never seen anything like it."

"It's a room Nancy built, so she could hold séances in it and speak to Don. It's pretty unbelievable. This room is probably worth more than all of the houses on this street put together. I have no idea if you can take gold leaf off of walls and sell it or whatever, but if you can, it would be worth a fortune."

Nancy was sobbing and through her sobs she said, "Don loves this room. His spirit is here. You have to leave it like it is for him. He'll be lost forever if it's changed."

"Mrs. Messinger," Roger said, "I'm no expert in matters like this, but from what I've heard Don is elsewhere and not in this room. It isn't going to make any difference to him what happens here, and the jail cell you're going to soon be in is definitely not going to be covered in gold leaf."

The sound of a siren neared, and they heard brakes screeching as the chief of police's car came to a stop in front of the house. It was quiet for a moment, and then the fat police chief yelled from the top of the stairs, "This is Police Chief Seth Williams. Who's down there?"

"It's okay, Seth. This is Roger Langley. Liz and I are down here and we're holding someone you need to arrest."

"Liz, Roger, I'm comin' down. Yer' safe now. Seth's here. Everything's gonna be okay." He waddled down the stairs, careful not to let the gravitational pull from the weight of his belly pull him forward and make him fall down the stairs.

When he got to the bottom he stopped and looked around in awe. "Ain't never seen nothin' like this." He turned and saw Roger aiming a gun at Nancy. "Well, I'll be durned. Don't this beat all. Uptight, snippety, better than everyone else Nancy Messinger got caught with her tootsie in the candy jar. Can't think of anyone I'd rather see in a cell than her. Always thought she was better than everyone else jes' because 'ol dead Don used to be the mayor of this here city. Soon's my deputy gets here, we'll take her in. Roger, what am I s'posed to charge her with?"

"First degree murder, attempted murder, and assault and battery. That ought to keep some lawyer busy for a while," Roger said. He looked over at Liz who was sitting on the floor with Winston's head in her lap. "Are you all right?"

"Barely, just barely. How did you know I was here?"

"Bob's mother-in-law overheard what you and Renee were planning to do this morning and became worried. She called Bob, and he immediately called me. He's on his way here. You probably better go upstairs and see how Renee's doing. Seth and I have this covered."

Liz walked up the stairs, carefully keeping a wide distance between Nancy and herself. As she left, she looked around the basement one more time in complete and total amazement. Winston followed her. She was half-way up the stairs when Roger said, "By the way, Liz, you promised me you would have your gun and Winston with you at all times. What happened?"

"Well, Roger. It's kind of like this. I told Nancy I had to go to the bathroom, so I left my purse in the living room. Thought it might look strange if I took it into the bathroom with me. As for Winston, guilty as your voice implies. I knew Nancy wouldn't let me bring him into her home, and I didn't want him sitting in Renee's car, so I decided to leave him at home. I know. I made a big mistake."

"It was not only a big mistake, it was almost a fatal mistake. When this is over, we might have to have a little talk about telling each other the truth about things, like where one is going when one goes out."

"You're right, Roger, you're absolutely right. Matter of fact, I had that same conversation with Renee this morning. I get it." She walked up the rest of the stairs and into the living room where Renee was sitting on the floor, shaking her head.

"What happened? I don't remember anything."

Liz filled her in on what had happened from the time Nancy hit her on the head with the butt of her pistol to now. There was a knock on the door. "Who is it?" Liz asked.

"Deputy Sims. Seth told me to meet him here, and I see his car out in front of the house."

Liz walked over to the door and opened it. "Everyone's downstairs, Deputy, and everything's under control," she said looking at the pistol in his hand. "The basement is through that door that's hanging by its hinges."

"Renee, how do you feel?" Liz asked, walking back to where Renee was sitting on the floor.

"My head is throbbing. I need to call Bob and tell him what's happened."

"Don't think that will be necessary. I believe that's his car that just pulled up. He's running up the sidewalk right now." Liz walked over to the door and opened it as Bob ran in.

"Oh, Renee. Are you all right? What happened?" he said, sitting down beside her and putting his arms around her.

"Bob, it's over." She started sobbing. "I'm all right. Nancy was the one who murdered Laura. I'm so glad mom called you. I don't know what would have happened if she hadn't. No, that's not true. I wouldn't be here right now, nor would Liz. We'd be dead."

"Oh, sweetheart, I'm so sorry this happened."

"So am I, but it's nothing you need to feel guilty about. It was a series of things that happened. Think about it. If Laura had opened that envelope instead of putting it in her coat pocket and forgetting about it, she'd still be alive. Plus, I wouldn't have a lump the size of a golf ball on my head, and we wouldn't have ruined Liz and Roger's honeymoon."

There was another knock on the door and Liz walked over and answered it. The older man standing in the doorway said, "I'm Jeff Gruber. Is everything all right?"

"Yes, it is now. Please come in."

He took one look at Renee and hurried over to her. "Renee, what happened? You know I'm a retired doctor, let me take a look at that lump on your head."

Jeff Gruber carefully felt it and assessed her vital signs as best he could without any medical equipment and said, "I think you're going to be fine. It's a nasty lump, but with the way your eyes are tracking I don't think you even have a concussion. You're lucky. What about Nancy?"

Renee told him what had happened. "I can't say I'm surprised," Jeff said. "She was always odd, and lately, had been even odder. I'm sorry for Laura. When you have some time I'd like to hear everything that led up to it. Where is everyone?"

"They're down in the basement," Renee said. "You might want to go down there and see where all the gold leaf went that she had delivered. I guess it's quite a sight to see."

"Renee, I'll be back in a minute, but I want to see this, too," Bob said and followed Jeff down the stairs.

A few minutes later, everyone came back up the stairs, Nancy in handcuffs with Deputy Sims walking behind her, his gun aimed at her back. Seth spoke, "Put her in the back of yer' squad car and take her to the slammer. Ya' got the wire screen in the car fer protection, and with her in handcuffs don't think ya' got a problem. I want to spend a minute with these fine folks. See ya' in a few."

He turned to Roger and the rest of the group. "Glad I was able to get here so fast and make sure all of ya' was safe. I can see that ya' are. Ya' never have to worry with me around as police chief. Liz, Roger, probably oughta get a statement from ya' when you have time. "You too," he said, nodding towards Renee. "Man, weren't that room the dangedest thing ya' ever seen? Kinda kinky, know what I mean? There's a lot I could do in that there room," he said smirking as he walked out the door.

Liz and Roger looked at each other and simply shook their heads. The others had a look of bewilderment on their faces as they tried to digest what Seth had just said. "Roger," Bob said, "am I missing something here? I thought you and Liz were the heroes. To hear that guy talk, he was."

"Bob, let's leave it that Seth is quite a complicated character. I think it's time you get Renee home. Obviously, she can't drive. We'll bring her car over tomorrow. Think Liz needs to get home as well. It's been a traumatic morning for all of us. Jeff, thank you. If you hadn't looked in that basement window, I would have lost precious time trying to figure out where Liz and Nancy were. Since this is the scene of a crime, I imagine at some point Seth will remember to cordon it off with yellow tape, so don't be surprised when someone shows up and does that. Okay, let's go."

They walked to their cars and waved to Jeff as they drove away. On the way back to the lodge, it was very apparent Winston knew exactly how much danger Liz had been in. He never stopped wagging his tail and covering Liz with wet sloppy dog kisses.

CHAPTER THIRTY-TWO

"Roger, we have a couple of days left before both of us have to get back to work," Liz said laughing. "Whoops! Maybe I should have said before we get back to work at our regular jobs. What we've gone through with Bob and Renee could definitely be considered work."

"You were so tired last night I didn't want to bother you, but I did hear from Jim. By the way, so much has happened, I almost forgot to tell you again how great that coq-au-vin was night before last. I know you've told me that cooking is therapy for you, so if you want to make it again in the next few days, that will be fine with me. We could both probably use a little comfort food."

"Thanks, and of course I'll make it again if you liked it that much. So, what did Jim say about Nick's arrest, although we can rule him out as the killer given Nancy's confession."

"He was arrested the morning of the murder, the morning of our wedding day. Kind of sad. Jim said the report from Serenity Center was very favorable, and the probation officer assigned to his case by the judge is hoping that instead of a prison sentence for being involved in a drug bust, maybe he could go back to Serenity. I told him about Laura, and he was going to personally tell Nick, probably as a favor to you for the case you helped him solve. Who knows? Maybe now that Nick doesn't have Laura as a reason to get clean, he'll do it for himself, which is really the only reason anyone should do it."

"I feel sorry for him. Any chance for a reconciliation is off the table, because there's no one to reconcile with. I don't know much about him, but I hope he has a family or some network that can give him support. He's going to need it. Next time you talk to Jim, ask him if he'd let us know if Nick is going to go back to Serenity. If he is, I'll call Mike and see if there's anything I can do."

"Rather you didn't, Liz. Think you've done your bit for that family. Nick will have to do this on his own. Matter of fact, I'm going to overrule that one."

"All right. I know you've been concerned about my safety. What about the Dear Reverend? He gets off completely, right? Actually, I guess there's nothing he can be charged with other than secretly drinking vodka out of a coffee cup and being hypocritical."

"Sweetheart, if being hypocritical was a crime, there would be so many people guilty of it the government would have to convert every inch of commercial property in the United States into prisons. In other words, if saying one thing and meaning another is hypocritical, some of us might not be any better than Reverend Jacobs," he said scowling at her.

"All right, all right. I get your message. I assume you mean that I was being hypocritical when I said I'd have Winston with me at all times, and then I didn't take him with me when I knew I was going to Nancy's. I suppose that's what you're getting at."

"Hypocritical, lying. Kind of one and the same thing in my mind. Neither one is a very good personality trait to have when you're beginning a marriage which is based on love and trust."

"No wonder you're such a good lawyer. You do have a way with words. Okay. Message received. One last thing. We can also scratch Candy and Mitch off the suspect list. Poor guy. I wonder if he'll ever get over Renee and recover from his depression."

"I have no idea, but we need to take Renee's car back to her today and go down to the station and give Seth a statement, but first I have a great idea. I never got a chance to carry you over the threshold of our bedroom. I'd kind of like to do that, being somewhat old-fashioned and all. Think I remember hearing it's considered to be good luck for a long marriage."

"Roger, why do I have a feeling you have an ulterior motive for doing that? I will tell you if you drop me, I will never forgive you."

"Well, my love, there's more than one way to skin a cat, so they say," he said lifting her up and throwing her over his shoulder in a fireman's carry. He winked at Winston as he walked down the hall with Liz over his shoulder who was laughing hysterically and yelling, "Roger, put me down."

Winston sighed and closed his eyes.

RECIPES

CASSOULET (CLASSIC FRENCH CASSEROLE DISH WITH BEANS, PORK CHOPS AND SAUSAGE

Ingredients

4 bone-in chicken thighs
1 tbsp. seasoning salt blend of choice
6 tbsp. olive oil, divided
2 boneless center-cut pork chops, cut into 8 pieces
6 oz. bacon
1 ½ medium onions, chopped
2 garlic cloves, peeled and diced
¾ cup chicken broth
1 ½ tbsp. tomato paste
Bouquet garni – bay leaf, celery stalk cut in two pieces, sprig of thyme (tie in a bundle)
¼ tsp. ground black pepper
½ tsp. pepper
15 oz. can great northern beans, drained
15 oz. can cannellini beans, drained
½ lb. Polish sausage, cut in ½ inch diagonal pieces
6 tbsp. minced fresh parsley plus 2 tsp. minced fresh thyme
½ cup of white wine or chicken broth, as needed

Directions

Preheat oven to 400 degrees. Mix parsley and thyme. Place 4 tablespoons of mixture in a dish with the rest in another dish. Season chicken thighs with seasoning salt on both sides. Place in a single layer in baking dish and bake for 45 minutes.

Put olive oil in deep ovenproof casserole. Add bacon and pork chops. Bake uncovered in preheated oven for 20 minutes. Turn once.

In a large skillet, heat remaining oil over medium heat. Add onions and cook until translucent. Add garlic and cook for one minute. Stir in broth, tomato paste, bouquet garni, salt, and pepper. Simmer, covered, for 2 minutes. Stir in beans and 4 tablespoons fresh herb mixture.

Remove chops and bacon from casserole, draining any excess oil. Pour half the bean mixture into casserole. Add bacon, chops, chicken thighs and sausage. Top with remaining bean mixture. If mixture seems too dry, you can add a little white wine or chicken broth.

Bake, uncovered, for 20-25 minutes. Remove and discard bouquet garni. Garnish with remaining fresh herb mixture. Enjoy!

STRAWBERRY ALMOND FLOUR CAKE

Ingredients

4 eggs, putting yolks and whites in separate bowls
½ cup sugar, divided
2 tbsp. sugar (for cake pan)
1 tsp. vanilla extract
1 ½ cups almond flour
1 tsp. baking powder
¼ tsp. salt
2 cups sliced strawberries
Optional: ice cream, chocolate sauce

Directions

Preheat oven to 350 degrees. Put a mixing bowl and electric mixer beaters in the freezer. Lightly grease an 8 inch round pan. Sprinkle 2 tbsp. sugar into the bottom and lower sides of the pan.

In a large mixing bowl whisk together the 4 egg yolks, ¼ cup sugar and vanilla.

In a separate bowl whisk together the almond flour, baking powder, and salt.

Remove the bowl and beaters from the freezer and put the egg whites in it. Beat the egg whites using an electric mixer. When they form soft peaks, add remaining ¼ cup sugar and incorporate into the egg whites.

Add the flour mixture to the egg yolk mixture. Add the egg whites (about ½ cup at a time) to the mixture. Pour the cake batter into the sugar coated cake pan and bake on center rack for 30 – 35 minutes. Remove from oven let cool in pan for 5 minutes. Run a knife around the edges to loosen the sides and turn the cake out onto a serving plate. Top with sliced strawberries in a circular pattern or one of your choosing. Might want a little ice cream or chocolate sauce with it. Enjoy!

COQ AU VIN (CHICKEN BRAISED IN RED WINE)

Ingredients
One 4-5 lb. roasting chicken, cut into 8 serving pieces (I usually substitute 8 chicken thighs)
8 oz. bacon
1 tsp. kosher salt
1 tsp. fresh ground pepper
1 large yellow onion, peeled and chopped
2 large carrots, peeled and chopped
2 large celery ribs, trimmed and chopped

1 leek, white and light green parts only, diced
3 tbsp. tomato paste
8 garlic cloves, peeled and diced
1/3 cup flour
1 bottle (750 ml) full bodied red wine, such as burgundy
2 – 3 cups chicken stock
2 tsp. fresh thyme leaves
1 bay leaf
2 tsp. cracked black peppercorns (I put them in a baggie and use a hammer)
18 pearl onion (I use frozen)
2 tbsp. unsalted butter
1 tbsp. vegetable oil
1 lb. crimini or white mushroom, bottom of stems sliced off & quartered
3 tbsp. fresh thyme leaves or parsley for garnish

Directions

Place bacon in a Dutch oven type pan and fry over moderate heat until crisp and fat has rendered, 8 – 10 minutes. Transfer bacon to a paper-towel lined plate. Season the chicken pieces on all sides with salt and pepper. Place chicken in pan and brown on all sides. Transfer chicken to baking sheet.

Add onions, carrots, celery, and leek to Dutch oven and cook until vegetables are browned, about 10 minutes. Add tomato paste and garlic and cook for 1 – 2 minutes. Sprinkle flour over the vegetable mixture and cook for 2 minutes, stirring constantly.

Add wine to the Dutch oven and scrape the bottom of the pan with a wooden spoon to release any browned bits. Cook 5 minutes. Put chicken and bacon in a slow cooker or crock pot. Add vegetable wine mixture and enough chicken stock to cover the chicken. Add thyme, bay leaves, and peppercorns stirring to combine. Cover the mixture and cook on medium for 4 – 5 hours. 1 hour before serving add the mushrooms and onions. Turn to low, if cooking a little too fast. Garnish with thyme leaves. If your slow cooker or crock pot won't hold all of it, divide in half and freeze for another time. Enjoy!

BISCUITS AND SAUSAGE GRAVY

Ingredients

1 lb. pkg. Mild Jimmy Dean Sausage (comes in a refrigerated plastic roll)
1 refrigerated roll ready to cook Hungry Man biscuits or similar brand
2 tbsp. ground sage
1 pint heavy cream
2 tbsp. Wondra flour
Salt and pepper to taste

Directions

Open the roll of sausage and with your fingers tear out <u>small</u> individual bite size pieces and place them in a 12" frying pan or electric skillet until the bottom of the pan is covered. OK to pack pieces in tight. Shake ground sage evenly over the sausage pieces. Turn heat to medium high and fry sausage, turning the individual pieces with tongs so all sides are evenly browned and cooked thoroughly.

If some pieces seem too large, use a pair of scissors to cut large pieces in half as they cook in the pan. When sausage is cooked, slide it to the side of the pan, turn down the heat to medium, and shake flour into the sausage grease and pan drippings, stirring to make a thin paste (1 min). Stir the sausage into the flour mixture so it covers the entire bottom of pan. Slowly add the cream (1/3 at a time). Stir constantly with a whisk or fork until a thick gravy is formed (approx. 3 minutes). If a thicker gravy is needed, add more flour, one teaspoon at a time until desired thickness of gravy is obtained. Add salt and pepper to taste. Turn heat to simmer.

Place the biscuits on a cookie sheet and bake according to package directions. When baked, remove biscuits from oven, split in half, and place on a dinner plate. Spoon the sausage gravy over the biscuits, completely covering them. Two fried eggs is a nice accompaniment. Serves 4. Enjoy!

EASY PEASY APPETIZER BITES (SEE NOTE)

Ingredients

1 can refrigerated pizza dough
4 slices bacon
½ cup grated mozzarella cheese
1 tbsp. diced green chilies
1 tbsp. sliced black olives
1 egg
1 tbsp. water

Directions

Preheat oven to 425 degrees. Spray cookie sheet with nonstick spray. Fry bacon over medium heat. Drain bacon pieces on paper towel lined plate. When cool, crumble. Make an egg wash by whisking the egg and water together in a small dish.

Tear off pieces of pizza dough into 2 inch squares. (Dough is very pliable so feel free to pull it out to the desired size.) Put a little bacon, cheese, chilies, and olives in center of dough and pinch ends together to close. Place pinched side down on prepared cookie sheet. When cookie sheet is filled, put remaining dough in plastic bag and return to refrigerator for a later use. It will hold for several days. Lightly brush egg wash mixture over tops of bites. Bake 10 – 12 minutes and remove from oven. Let rest for 2 minutes and place on plate for guests. Enjoy!

NOTE: This is about the most forgiving thing I've ever cooked. You can fill them with whatever's in your refrigerator or pantry. Feel free to exchange the mozzarella cheese with whatever cheese you have on hand. Bacon can be replaced with any cooked leftover meat. Jams, jellies, there are no rules here. Play and have fun. <u>Caution</u>: Be prepared to make another batch because people LOVE them!

Three Amazing Ebooks & Seven Paperbacks for FREE

Go to www.dianneharman.com/freepaperback.html and get your FREE copy of Kelly's Coffee Shop, Blue Coyote Motel and Dianne's favorite recipes immediately by joining her newsletter.

Once you join her newsletter you're eligible to win seven autographed paperbacks from the Cedar Bay Cozy Mystery Series. One lucky winner is picked every week. Hurry before the offer ends.

ABOUT THE AUTHOR

Dianne lives in Huntington Beach, California with her husband Tom, a former California State Senator, and her boxer puppy, Kelly. Her passions are cooking and dogs, so whenever she has a little free time, you can find her in the kitchen or in the back yard throwing a ball for Kelly. She is a frequent contributor to the Huffington Post.

Her other award winning books include:

Cedar Bay Cozy Mystery Series
Kelly's Koffee Shop, Murder at Jade Cove, White Cloud Retreat, Marriage and Murder, Murder in the Pearl District, Murder in Calico Gold, Murder at the Cooking School

Liz Lucas Cozy Mystery Series
Murder in Cottage #6, Murder & Brandy Boy, The Death Card, Murder at The Bed & Breakfast

High Desert Cozy Mystery Series
Murder & The Monkey Band

Coyote Series
Blue Coyote Motel, Coyote in Provence, Cornered Coyote

Website: www.dianneharman.com
Blog: www.dianneharman.com/blog
Email: dianne@dianneharman.com

Newsletter
If you would like to be notified of her latest releases please go to www.dianneharman.com and sign up for her newsletter.

CPSIA information can be obtained
at www.ICGtesting.com
Printed in the USA
FSOW01n2325100716
22563FS